MURDER'S
A WAITING GAME

MURDER'S
A WAITING GAME

by Anthony Gilbert

Random House: New York

Library of Congress Cataloging in Publication Data

Malleson, Lucy Beatrice, 1899-
Murder's a waiting game.

I. Title.
PZ3.M2943Mum3 [*PR6025.A438*] *823'.9'12* *75-37039*
ISBN 0-394-47933-5

9 8 7 6 5 4 3 2

Manufactured in the United States of America
by The Colonial Press, Clinton, Mass.

MURDER'S
A WAITING GAME

1

The card was enclosed in an envelope so thin and mean that I was tempted to drop it straight into the wastepaper basket. Just another advertisement offering a free lipstick if you buy ten pounds' worth of cosmetics, I thought. Idly I slit the flap.

I was staring, the past running by like water from a forgotten tap. The card itself was as cheap as its cover, bearing neither address nor signature. The message, printed in black capitals, read:

CONGRATULATIONS, MRS. FIELDING, FOR MAKING SUCH A GRAND COMEBACK. IF YOU WOULD LIKE TO ACQUIRE THE FINAL BIT OF EVIDENCE TO MAKE YOUR SITUATION WATERTIGHT, BE AT THE TEAPOT AND DORMOUSE AT 6 P.M. TOMORROW NIGHT.

The crudity of the thing astounded me, though I didn't know what it meant. The final bit of evidence . . .

I put a hand over my eyes, thinking, as one does in moments of crisis, This can't be true, it's a dream, in a minute I'll wake up and everything will be normal again. I shall see the gold-and-white curtains blowing in the windows, the Canaletti print hanging above the lowboy, the plate of glorious colors we'd brought back from Vienna and the little carved Florentine angel that had come from the market near the Uffizi. The card would be part of a momentary nightmare.

But when I looked down, there it still lay in my lap, something threatening that had broken through a weak place I hadn't known existed.

My first thought now was how fortunate it was I had the house to myself for the next two or three days. My husband was defending a case at the Liverpool Assizes. Under his penetrating gaze I doubted whether I could keep up appearances. (It never occurred to me I might show him the card.) My second thought was, Why *now?* Ten years ago, when the Harding case was filling the papers, or even two years later when I remarried, yes, perhaps; but not ten years later, when I believed I'd really buried the past and my life was as new as though swinging round a fresh corner, I'd walked into a different world. That very morning I'd said goodbye to our son, Gavin, setting out for his first school, then Aubrey had departed, and I had come home, thinking, If only something would happen to take my mind off the bleakness of the house, with both husband and son away. Well, here was something with a vengeance, and my last state was worse than my first.

I forgot about lunch—this was the day our domestic help went off at twelve o'clock—just sat like some stone figure Rodin might have carved, only I hadn't that figure's spring of living. The house was silent and empty about me, no one would be coming in before morning. The years fell away like ashes or dust, and I was back in the world I thought I'd put behind me ten years ago.

I was born Margaret Cooper, and when the aunt who had brought me up unexpectedly married, when I was seventeen, a man a dozen years her junior, I realized fast enough there wasn't room for the three of us under the same roof. My new uncle, Noel, who couldn't have been much over thirty, said effusively that in getting a wife he had also got himself a daughter, but his manner toward me was anything but fatherly. So, having no means of my own, and my aunt's income being severely telescoped now she had a husband to support, I got myself a job with Sebastian, the photographer. He wasn't the great name he has since become, but he had an ambition as high as Everest even then. He was a dark-haired, rather pale-skinned man in his early thirties, dear Uncle Noel's contemporary, I thought—and in those days he operated in a cramped studio in Baker Street.

I was what is now called a Girl Friday, an odds-and-sods girl, Uncle Noel said. I got to the studio at nine o'clock and the day ended with the day's work. It might be seven or eight or later, I doubt if Sebastian had ever heard of overtime; he had no home life that I ever discovered. His work was his whole existence. Nowadays, of course, he's one of the really great names in his profession, then he was on his way up, and it was my privilege to do anything required of me, and it was as a privilege that I saw it. I made the appointments, tidied the studio, fobbed off the cadgers, the odd salesmen, the self-advertisers, and after my first year was sometimes allowed to take a picture myself. These were always signed Sebastian Studios. Only photos he had actually taken were signed with his own name.

My first subject was a social-climbing mama, with a revoltingly coy small child—but that's beside the point, except that she expressed delight at the result, qualifying her remarks by the observation that no one could hope to do her angel justice. The picture I took that changed my whole life was one of a dog, a large, silly, amiable Dalmatian called Aristo. "Short for Aristocratic. My Mama has a splendid sense of humor," said the young man who brought him in. Sebastian never photographed dogs, though he'd done some lovely studies of cats, all fluid grace and independence. He didn't like dogs, but he didn't object to my taking over the commission. The dog's owner lived in Cadogan Square and price was no object. The dog's guard was a bit miffed when he found Sebastian wouldn't sign the work in person. "My Mama would be tickled pink to see that signature," he urged. But in the end he capitulated. "She's so scatty she probably won't appreciate the difference," he said. "Anyway, in Italy they probably won't know."

The Dalmatian sat and beamed at us both. His guard— that's how he referred to himself, "he's not mine, I'm privileged to walk him, that's all"—told me, "My Mama only wants to get me off her hands, and then she's off to Italy with Aristo. No absurd quarantine laws there, you see."

Aristo proved a most amenable subject. He hadn't much change of expression, but at all events, he didn't try and show off like a poodle or express character like a terrier. He just sat and beamed. Having him about the house, I thought, would be like living in a land of perpetual sun. One might even get sunstroke.

We sent Derek Harding the proofs and he came in to discuss them, and came again to collect the finished article. On the last occasion he suggested casually I might like to come out with him to dine and dance one evening. I went. Derek was a lovely dancer. He had a cherishing way of holding his partner, and needless to say, he had charm, even more charm than Uncle Noel. It oozed out of his ears. A little later I met his mother, who looked like a marquise, and who seemed to take to me at sight. All the same, I was a bit taken aback when Derek proposed.

"The sort of daughter-in-law my Mam's been looking for for years," he declared enthusiastically. It wasn't perhaps quite the usual recommendation, but then I'd been swept off my feet, too, by her magnetism. The pair of them were irresistible, and a few months after our first meeting I found myself in a church I'd never entered before being made into the wife of a man I scarcely knew.

I didn't understand about that till we'd been married for some time. For all his apparent openness of manner, Derek was really a rather secretive person. I knew he had a job of sorts, but he never went into much detail. Sales rep, for a firm making engineering products was the nearest I got. I wasn't lonely at first. I had the house to care for, and I never minded going around on my own discovering London—I hadn't made many friends while working with Sebastian because he took every scrap of energy I had. I had expected Derek to bring people home, other newly married men with wives of my own age, but he never did. "Enough shop by day," he would observe, "now for a little light relief." During that first year he was very attentive, we went out a good deal, more, I realized later, than he could possibly afford. My only real disappointment was that I had no prospect of a child. By the second year I began to be apologetic.

"Oh, stuff it, Maggie," Derek said. "What's so marvelous about being pregnant anyway? The birds and the bees do it all the time, and are we not much greater than they?"

When I realized he didn't want a child, would have been shocked to find himself cast in the role of a father—he hated responsibility and even he couldn't have expected a child to fend for itself—I changed a bit too. It was during the second year I realized he wasn't completely faithful. I never made the mistake of thinking this was the sort of thing that can break up a marriage—a scented note signed Daisy left, with typical carelessness, in a raincoat pocket. I'd seen the way women looked at him, and the way he looked back—and how were they to know it meant nothing to him? I burned the note and sent the raincoat to the cleaners, as he'd asked me to do.

Then during the third year, at the very beginning of it, he came in, smiling and gay, to tell me this was a great occasion, he'd cast his vote for independence—his way of telling me he'd lost his job.

"You never saw a man so surprised in his life as old Pringle," he confided. "Jaw fell so far he had to stoop down and pick it up from the carpet."

Typically he had brought a bottle of champagne to celebrate.

"What now?" I asked.

"Let a man breathe. Plenty of cozy corners if you know where to look for them."

Before he'd found his, ten weeks later, I'd decided I'd had enough of domesticity in isolation and got myself a job working for a beautician. Two or three weeks later Derek was signed on as buyer for a firm of pharmaceutical chemists. He had to do a good deal of traveling—taking the good news to the ends of the earth, he called it. "Pity we can't change places." He grinned. "You could soften my hard-faced old men and I'd bewitch your lovelies."

"Oh, they're tougher than they look," I assured him.

It wouldn't be true to say I wasn't happy, even at that stage. I liked my job, I liked meeting different people and having more money to spend. Derek seemed cheerful, too; I supposed the job was going well. Now and again I wondered what he did with himself when he was away from home, staying in some overnight hotel, but I didn't fancy he lacked for company. And he never showed any suspicion of my activities. I genuinely don't believe it would have occurred to him that anyone married to Derek Harding would be tempted to stray.

The following year his mother was killed in a car crash in Italy, and he took it desperately hard.

"I was fond of the old girl," he said. "She was as mad as a hatter, I know, but she was awfully good fun. And it was really her behind our marriage."

He'd never spoken so candidly before. "You mean, you . . ."

"Of course I wanted to marry you," he said impatiently. "But you were the first one she approved, and goodness knows, she had choice enough. I couldn't have married anyone she didn't like."

He flew over for the funeral, and when he came back he seemed more dependent than before. I hadn't guessed how much he relied on her. I wondered if she'd helped him out with money.

He paid me more attention than he'd done for months. "You stick to me, old girl," he said once. "The others, they're like cigarettes, a spit and a puff, but you're for real. I never wanted to marry any of the others."

Oddly enough, I believed that, but it disturbed me that he could so openly admit the existence of the others. I consoled myself with the reflection that if they had had any real significance for him he wouldn't have mentioned them at all.

Neither of us at this time would have believed that in less than two years I should be standing my trial for his murder.

Some weeks after Mrs. Harding's death I, too, changed my job, going in with a publishing combine, working on their publicity staff. Through them I met Tom Cribbins.

Tom, in certain ways, reminded me of Sebastian. He looked rather like him. He had the same blazing enthusiasm, the single-minded drive. He did a lot of reading for Willis, my new employers, and shortly afterward became one of their editors. He confided to me he'd like to publish his own list, but he realized that was out of the question. The publishing houses had fallen into step with the banks and big business in general —amalgamate, amalgamate, was their cry. This was a period when Derek often didn't get back at night. He'd telephone long distance—another fuggy hotel, he'd say.

I never could pin him down precisely to what he did these days, but I never felt much security either. The most secure thing in my life was my job. That would endure when personal relationships failed. Charm can carry you a long way if you're in the right situation, but it's weightless, you need something to drag it back to earth. I began to take advantage of his constant absences, made a few friends locally, and others at work, and among them was Tom Cribbins. It became quite normal for us during those months to go out together, have something to eat, go to a cinema—he was unmarried and foot-loose—even the occasional concert, though I wasn't specially musically minded. I never took him home, and if he had a home he never spoke of it. He seemed as free as a bird that settles on tree after tree, but nests and rests nowhere.

Since I'd started work we'd had a woman whom Derek would call the hausfrau. She was a Hungarian who had escaped with several members of her family during the 1956 rising; she hadn't been so fortunate as most of them, who had managed to reach the States, but she still cherished the notion that she would get there eventually, kept up with her family and showed me splendidly elaborate cards she received at Christmas. She was perpetually telling us—telling me, actually, since Derek never listened—about liberty in the freest country in the world. I should have expected her to be pleased that I was out so often in the evenings when Derek was away, since our arrangement allowed for two hours' employment at night, and she had little enough to do from six to eight, when she was due to go home.

Yes, if I'd given the matter a thought I'd have expected her to like me, rather than the reverse. But as events were to show, she proved one of my worst enemies.

I was twenty-three and four years married when Tom's chance came. He'd been to the States on Willis' business and come back cock-a-hoop. A man called Aden was opening a literary agency and wanted Tom to handle the English books. "And, of course," Tom pointed out, his voice choked with pleasure, "there are my continental connections. This is the chance I've looked for for years."

He handed in his notice as soon as he got back.

I rejoiced with him—naturally. It's impossible not to, when a friend gets his heart's desire, but I was simultaneously aware of the comparative dullness of my life when Tom had gone out of it. Of course, I had other friends, but none of them would make up for his loss.

"I'm glad for you, truly I am," I said. "It's what you've always wanted." In a sense, it was all he wanted. "I'm going to miss you, though," I added candidly.

He put his hand over mine. "Jealous, Maggie?"

"What do you think?"

I saw myself going on in the same rut year after year. I'd never get one of the plums. You need to be free for that. I couldn't have gone to America for three weeks as Tom had done. Some husbands would have agreed, but not Derek. His manner had been oddly defensive lately. I wondered if he was on the verge of losing this job, too. I knew anything that came his way now would be less than promotion. He was like one of those days that start in golden glory, cloud over, chill and end in torrents of rain. He wasn't near the torrents yet, but I could glimpse them ahead. He was still handsome, could exert charm when he pleased, though this was less often than formerly, but he was getting flabby, played no sports, went everywhere by car.

"What made you marry that stuffed shirt?" asked Tom unexpectedly. "You must have been pretty young to be misled by the picture in the window. I suppose he represented a place in society, a house with mod cons . . ."

"Those weren't my reasons," I protested, but Tom swept over me like a storm.

"Even at nineteen you must have known nothing is for free."

"I wanted to marry him," I insisted. "If I'd only wanted a roof, I could pay for that myself."

I had a fleeting vision of the marriage I'd intended to make. A new start, a place in a different society, a husband beside me, a society where we were a married couple, with children, of course, a stake in the future. I'd been thinking Derek

11

hadn't made much of a success of things. I hadn't done so much better myself. Within four years or so we were occupying separate rooms. Derek said his hours were so elastic it would be more restful for me, and he had taken over the room I'd set aside for a nursery. He never seemed to realize the humiliation this involved for me. Not that he neglected me, but I felt another plank in our marriage platform had gone.

"Yes," I said thoughtfully, "I wanted Derek—then."

"Ever thought about a divorce?" Tom asked casually.

I'd sometimes dreamed of freedom, but I'd always bypassed the way I could attain it. I certainly didn't want Derek to die, I just wanted a chance to start again, the sort of chance Tom now had.

"Not really," I said. "Derek wouldn't agree, anyway."

"How can you be so sure?"

"Because if he'd wanted it he'd have told me."

"Does the choice have to rest with him?" Tom asked. "You're a big girl now, Maggie. What do you suppose he does in the evenings when he doesn't come home? Play tiddly-winks by himself in a hotel bedder? The man's human, isn't he?"

The idea, once planted in my mind, took root like a seed in earth. But I only had to breathe the word to Derek for the balloon to go up in flames.

"Over my dead body," he said. "Till death doth us part. Remember?"

I remembered taking that oath without a qualm. My only fear had been that death might part us all too soon. Now I had a different vision of the future. Year by year life would sweep past me, while I, like a paraplegic or someone on crutches, got left behind in the wake. I never wanted to take up Tom Cribbins' challenge as I did that night . . .

The door opened crisply and Etta came in. "You want dinner?" she demanded.

"I'll come and dish up," I said. It occurred to me as I did

12

so that it was ages since Derek and I had had one of those easy domestic conversations that come naturally to most married couples.

I wondered, though, if the suggestion had had an unexpected effect, because not long afterward Derek told me his firm was drawing in its horns, covering a smaller area. "There's a vacancy nearer home," he said, "and I've put in for it. You won't need to play the grass widow any longer." I hoped that really was the way of it. I thought that a man who was making good with a firm would be given an enlarging job, not one contained in a much smaller area.

Tom went to America, whence he sent me a long, enthusiastic letter, then a second entirely devoted to his new work. I answered both, but temporarily. I felt he'd moved into another planet. I saw more of Derek, but we seemed to have lost the capacity for casual homemaking. He said he was too fagged out to want to play bridge or listen to intellectual conversation. He liked to plant himself in front of the television set. Sometimes he came in later, enraging Etta, who seemed to live by the clock. Had to wait and see a man, he'd tell me. He didn't have to add that most of the meeting was done in a bar. He was never less than sober, but there's a difference between the sobriety of a man who's taken nothing and another man who's had a couple or so.

Then I heard through someone at the office that Tom was engaged to a girl called Rosamund Something. Just before I got the news I'd succumbed to a mood of frightful depression; my own future seemed devoid of hope. I hardly even got companionship from Derek any more, and the office had lost more than half its charm since Tom went. I began to write to him, pouring out my heart, as the romantic novelists say. I don't know even now that I was really in love with him, not as I came to know love in later years, but he'd become essential to my days, like a door into a new world, and now the door had clanged shut. I'd been surprised at the way his resignation had been accepted. I thought they'd have given a big farewell party for him, but everything went off very coolly. I think there was a general feeling that he'd let them down by going at such short notice. But none of those who remained could make up to me for Tom.

I remember some of the phrases I wrote. Derek will never agree to a divorce, I shall be hamstrung here for the rest of my days. Sometimes I wish these were the Middle Ages when magic could still be invoked. Long before I finished writing it I knew I wouldn't send it. I suppose that should have warned me how tenuous was my hold on him. I crumpled it up and threw it in the wastepaper basket, but in a way I felt better for having written it. When I got the news about Rosamund, I burned at the thought that I might actually have posted it. I went on with my job, Derek went on with his. Now and again he talked of it in a vague way, old So-and-So was a nutter, if *he* had X's job he'd put the firm on the map all right. Just words, words, I thought.

"I'll surprise you all yet," he declared. And so indeed he did.

He got more publicity for his death than he'd ever got out of living.

2

On the day he died Derek came back late for dinner. It irked him that we had to keep nursery hours to suit Etta, who fidgeted so if she was kept even a few minutes after eight that I wondered whether she ran a sensational private life; but since she wasn't an *au pair* girl her morals were no concern of mine.

That evening we were having jugged hare, which Derek particularly liked. I cooked it, with Etta at my elbow telling me of the superior culinary methods of her native land, but as she had left there as quite a young child I didn't pay much attention to her. The only dish she could cook properly was scrambled eggs. In America, she assured me, eggs were always eaten scrambled. Also she made very good coffee. Everything else was left to me.

By seven-fifteen there was no sign of Derek.

"Perhaps he was in an accident," suggested Etta with a sort of grim delight.

More likely to be in a bar, I thought. That's where you put up the orders, he used to tell you. I thought his must be a very peculiar firm.

At seven-twenty he rang to say he'd be a bit late, but was on his way. I hung up the receiver, wondering just what the trouble was. Something to do with his job? Only he usually adopted a jaunty tone where his work was concerned, and he certainly didn't sound jaunty tonight. He sounded—what? Deflated, like a man who's missed a bus and knows there won't be another, not in time, anyhow, to serve his purpose. I went into the dining room and put out a bottle of wine. I don't think he knew very much about wine, but he said it was civilized, and if he was really feeling dejected it might cheer him up. Etta brought the sherry into the study, the room where he did what he called his paperwork when he was at home.

When Derek came in, his appearance matched his telephone voice. "God, I'm bushed," he said.

Etta appeared at my shoulder. "I serve dinner?"

"Give us a chance," said Derek. He went into the study, and I poured us each a glass of sherry. He swallowed his almost at a gulp. "I needed that," he said, holding out his glass for a refill. But I wondered; it looked to me as if he might have had enough already.

I picked up my glass. "Bad day?" I asked. I could hear a note of genuine sympathy in my voice. His own word described him—bushed. I couldn't see why things should ever improve for him.

In the kitchen Etta was dropping spoons to remind us of the time.

"Lazy bitch!" said Derek. "Think of all the evenings when she's got nothing to do but sit on her fanny and carry on with her boyfriend on our phone. I daresay you don't have many solitary evenings when I'm not around."

I let that ride. I got the impression he hardly knew what he was saying. So it was the job, I decided. That was always my first thought, and I was usually right.

In the kitchen Etta clashed saucepans. "The hare will be ruined," I said pacifically. Not that I felt calm. If he really was leaving this job it was goodbye to all my hopes of a divorce. I couldn't walk out on him and leave him flat. We'd never discussed the subject again, but I thought about it often as children think of some treat that's bound to come their way *tomorrow*.

We came into the dining room. Etta planked the hare down on the table. She must have turned up the oven, because it was notably leathery. Derek opened the wine and filled both our glasses, we helped ourselves to hare, Etta slammed out.

"Had to see a man about a dog," elaborated Derek. "Kept me a while—might do us both a bit of good, though. Worth one overcooked hare."

I smiled and lifted my glass. "Big deal," I said.

Though hare was one of his favorite dishes, tonight he didn't seem to have much appetite. He accepted a second helping as much to irritate Etta as because he really wanted it. We'd just started on the trifle when the phone rang. I pushed back my chair.

"I'll take it," said Derek quickly.

Such alacrity was most unusual in him: I wondered if he had been expecting a call and knew who was on the other end.

We had one instrument in the hall, and an extension in the bedroom we used to share. I thought it might be Lucy Foster ringing me up about the upholstery class we had both joined. It filled in an otherwise empty evening for me, and I found myself resenting the possibility that Derek would try to prevent my going. I sighed, picked up the wine bottle and topped both our glasses. I heard the faint tinkle of the phone bell as he put the receiver down, then he came back, a rather sardonic grin on his face.

"That girl of yours" (he meant Etta) "must have been a tape recorder in a previous existence. Hover, hover, like some bloody great bee. It was for you, by the way," he added, taking his place at the table. "I've got the number. The sooner your chums realize that I don't care for this American bar habit of ringing up at mealtimes, the better."

"Probably thought we should have finished by now," I murmured.

When he stood up at last he said, "Tell that wench to bring the coffee to the den."

It always exasperated me to hear him call his study the den. Foxes have dens; thieves have dens; Daniel was in a lions' den but not from choice. I called out to Etta, who flung open the door dramatically. She was a tall, sallow girl looking more than her twenty-five years, with black caterpillars of hair falling over a bony forehead, but in her own way, not undistinguished. I put away the silver cruets and replaced the table mats. I went along to the study, and Derek and I drank coffee amicably, like any ordinary husband and wife. Presently I telephoned Lucy Foster. It was a pleasure to hear her gay, comfortable voice. I explained about Derek, apparently planning to spend all his evenings at home, and she said easily, "Well, tell him to have dinner at his club that night, and if he hasn't got one, to take his girl friend out. He'll have one of those, they all do."

After I'd hung up and gone back to the room Etta would call the lounge, the house seemed very quiet. Derek was stopping in his "den." Etta had splashed through the washing-up and I heard the back door close. She always came in by the front using her own key, but she liked to slip out by the back way at night. I found myself wishing we had an animal, a dog or a cat—but who'd look after that when we were both at work? Not Etta. She disliked animals, thinking it unnatural for them to be under the same roof as human beings. I got up and turned on the television. A little later Derek put his head in to say, "I'm off," and he repeated, "I'm bushed." I was shocked to think that a man of thirty-two could look so old and out of the race. I watched a program about maladjusted children, and wondered how the mothers ever got accustomed to their situation.

When at last I went upstairs, the house was as quiet as death. I thought, What a trite metaphor! But what can be more silent? I pulled back the curtain and saw the slender moon with a single star, like a backcloth. All my similes tonight seemed to be theatrical ones. I found myself wishing I was back at eighteen, inexperienced and free. I stood there a long time, looking at the marvelous sky, thinking about the fu-

ture, for once thinking more about Derek's than my own.
What future could *he* anticipate? At last I let the curtain fall
and dropped into bed.

In the early days of our marriage Derek had bought me a
Teasmaid. We both enjoyed a cup in bed, but neither of us felt
energetic enough to go downstairs, particularly on winter
mornings, to put on a kettle. If only we had a flat, I used to
moan sometimes. No long, cold stairs . . . So one evening
Derek surprised me by turning up in a taxi with the Teasmaid
under his arm. Even though we now occupied separate rooms,
I still carried him a cup of tea first thing; and I did this the
morning after Lucy Foster's call. Derek was still asleep. I put
the tea down and pulled back the curtain to let in the golden
day.

"Wake up, sleepyhead," I warned him. "The tea'll be
cold."

He didn't move, so I stooped to wake him: and I couldn't
do it, I couldn't do it, my own husband. So last night hadn't
been an act, after all. "I'm bushed," he'd said. And now this,
extinguished like a light. I never had any doubt that he was
dead.

Shock kept me calm, too calm perhaps. I stood beside the
bed, not hearing even the aggressive ticking of Derek's alarm
clock, trying to make myself realize I wouldn't be seeing or
hearing him again. I remembered last night wishing I could go
backward in time and achieve freedom, but I had never supposed it would come in this fashion. As for his future, there
was no need to speculate about that any more.

It was Etta's decisive slam of the front door that brought
me back to reality. I looked at the clock. What time had I
come in carrying the unwanted cup? I couldn't now be certain,
time seemed to have lost all sense, but the tea had scummed
over. I realized I should have done something before this, telephoned a doctor, at least. I didn't know our panel doctor very

well—neither of us had a private physician. We had both enjoyed good health, and I supposed it was about eighteen months since either of us had seen him. It didn't occur to me that Derek might have seen another doctor when he was away from home. I had to look up Dr. Fletcher's telephone number, we used it so seldom, and while I waited I heard the shrill running of the kitchen tap, and knew that Etta was making the cup of tea with which she started the day's work. I heard the busy signal, and went on to the landing.

"Etta!" I called imperiously.

She came sulkily as far as the kitchen door. I couldn't see her as yet, but you could tell her moods by her movements.

"Mr. Harding's been taken ill," I said. "I'm ringing the doctor. Be ready to let him in."

"Perhaps he eat too much hare," offered Etta unsympathetically.

"There was nothing wrong with the hare. We all had it."

"I do not feel too good," said Etta.

"I'm ringing Dr. Fletcher now," I said.

This time I got a reply, but it was Mrs. Fletcher who answered, in the slightly indignant tones of a doctor's wife who knows her husband is overworked and unappreciated, telling me he had been called out to a premature birth.

"These expectant mothers," she said. "Can't get themselves to hospital at the right time. She was warned there might be complications. How urgent is it?" she added. I presumed that by now she had switched her interest to Derek.

"He isn't conscious," I said. "I can't rouse him. I think he's pretty bad." I couldn't bring myself to say the fatal word.

"Try Dr. Gardner," Mrs. Fletcher advised me. "He stands in for my husband in emergencies, and vice versa."

My second call was also answered by a woman, this time telling me her husband was unavailable because he was in bed with pleurisy. Again I was asked how urgent the case was.

"Exceedingly urgent," I said. "He's not conscious, and it's not just a faint."

"Temperature?"

"I can't take that," I said, appalled.

"Better ring for an ambulance." She gave me a number. "If you explain . . ."

The ambulance came quite soon, but when they heard there was no doctor's advice they said they couldn't move the patient.

"You can't do him any harm," I said recklessly.

"That's for the doctor to say, love."

"But I can't get a doctor," I protested. "One's out at a premature birth and the other's in bed and wanting a doctor himself."

The second ambulance man said, "Wasn't that a doctor's plate at the end of the road, Bert?" and I said yes, that was Dr. Thurlow, but he only had private patients. Then, catching the glance they exchanged, I said, "Of course, I'd be prepared to pay him if he'd come. But what makes you think he would?"

"May as well find out," said the driver philosophically.

Etta poked her head around the door to know if she should bring coffee. "Not for us, love," said the man who'd suggested Dr. Thurlow. "I expect you've got plenty to do."

Even at this crisis the sight of Etta's outraged face made me laugh—almost. The driver accompanied me to the corner house; it was he who explained the situation. I suppose it was one with which Dr. Thurlow was fairly familiar. I think it was the ambulance uniform that tipped the scales.

"I have patients coming along shortly," Dr. Thurlow said, "but as soon as my assistant arrives I'll send him along."

Etta was carefully dusting the sitting room when we got back. The second ambulance man was ostentatiously reading the racing selections. As we came in I heard him say, "Well, no one can complain the cat's got your tongue, can they?"

21

Dr. Faulds arrived sooner than I anticipated. I told him rather jerkily what had happened. I thought he'd ask a lot of questions, but he didn't, just told me Derek's own doctor should be informed as soon as possible. The ambulance men loaded Derek onto a stretcher and we all drove off to the hospital.

Etta had tried to stop us even in the hall. "If anyone ring up, what do I say?"

It was one of the ambulance men who answered. "Ask a daft question," he said. "The boss is sick and gone to hospital, ring up later when Mrs. Harding might be home."

I had watched Derek being put on the stretcher; I hadn't waited with him till the doctor came, there was no point, and I didn't want to give Etta too free a field. Goodness only knows what she might be saying. At the hospital I was put to wait in the still-empty casualty corridor. I felt a burning desire for coffee, but it was too early for the hospital canteen to be open and I dared not leave the premises and go to a cafeteria across the road. Hanging on the wall opposite me was a Lowry print —"The Fever Van." I wondered who had thought that suitable for a casualty department, or if it was the gift of a grateful patient. It wasn't very long before a nurse told me Dr. Tewkesbury would like a word with me.

Dr. Tewkesbury was a bullet-headed young man looking older than casualty doctors normally do, who didn't believe in frills.

"You've seen your husband, Mrs. Harding," he said. "I'm sure you appreciate there's nothing we can do for him."

"I didn't know, for certain," I stammered. "But why? Why? He said he was bushed and he did seem tired, but he ate and drank as usual. But . . ."

"But what, Mrs. Harding?"

"Men don't die—that's what you mean, isn't it?—because they're bushed. He never suffered from a weak heart, at least not so far as either of us knew."

"He didn't die of heart disease," said Dr. Tewkesbury dryly.

"Then what?"

"In my opinion he died of an overdose of barbiturates."

"But that's absurd," I cried, before I could stop myself. "He never even took the stuff, if you mean sleeping tablets, as I suppose you do."

"Would you know?" he asked, and I felt myself blushing.

"We'd been occupying separate rooms while his hours were so elastic," I acknowledged, "but he'd have told me. Anyway, he hadn't seen our doctor."

"He could have seen another doctor."

"I must have known," I insisted. I thought of Derek's room, nothing ever put away, no cupboard doors closed.

"Yes, well, that'll be a point for the coroner to raise," Dr. Tewkesbury said. He wasn't precisely unsympathetic, but the first casualties of the day were seeping in, he might have two, three, four serious accidents before lunch. And Derek wasn't his affair any longer.

All the same I couldn't stop myself saying, "The coroner?"

"Where death isn't due to natural causes, a report has to be made to the coroner's office and he'll institute inquiries. It's just routine, Mrs. Harding. Now you go home . . . is there anyone there?"

I explained about Etta.

"No relations?" I shook my head. "Neighbors?"

But I didn't want them. When the whisper went around that the coroner was being invoked, they'd be around in their teeming hundreds.

"No breakfast, I suppose?" Dr. Tewkesbury said.

I shook my head. "Well—a cup of tea."

"Tell that girl of yours to make you a pot of coffee, and eat something, that's important, you're going to need your strength. You're going to be asked quite a lot of questions—that's inevitable."

I gathered from his manner that he thought I might be going to learn quite a lot, too. He'd got us taped as one of those inadequate couples who can't make a go of it. I resented his assurance. "I ought to be at work," I discovered suddenly.

"Not today," said the doctor. "Did you take in what I said about questioning?"

"Do you mean the police?"

He stared. "Well, who else? This is an unexplained death. If you've any explanation that you haven't offered me, don't imagine they won't uncover it. In any case, it's to your advantage as well as theirs to find out the truth."

"I don't see that," I said. "It can't be to Derek's advantage, since he's out of it all. This sort of publicity can't do me any good or bring him back. You know what he died of . . ."

"Talk sense, Mrs. Harding," he said harshly. "On that showing, any death could pass unquestioned."

"You're going to try and establish he committed suicide, aren't you? And he not there to speak for himself. I've told you already, that's the last thing he'd do. Besides, don't they always leave a letter?"

"That depends on how easy they want to make things for the survivors. And if I may give you a word of advice—the shock has blunted your judgment, I daresay, it often happens—think twice before you make any runaway statements. What the police look for aren't theories, but proof. And if you haven't any, leave it to them to find it. You'll be told the date of the inquest, and naturally you'll be expected to attend. If you're perplexed you could talk to your lawyer."

He gave a sort of jerk and went away. I realized rather belatedly that he intended to be sympathetic. Perhaps at that time he saw a great deal further than I did. All the same, I was the one who knew Derek. He wouldn't take the stuff himself, wouldn't know where to get it—or would he? He traveled for this pharmaceutical firm—but would that give him access to drugs? Surely they're controlled by the Home Office or the British Medical Association. I was shocked to realize how little I knew about my husband's work. But he'd never spoken of it, except to say once that Gully was a grasping old sod. Only shop in working hours, he used to say. Let the muck lie till morning. Somehow it was more than pathetic, it was almost heartbreaking that he should have known so little of delight in work during his two-and-thirty years.

As I came out of the hospital another ambulance drew up and a policeman jumped out, with a most elegantly rolled umbrella on his arm. I don't know why it seemed so funny; it made me think of a musical show Derek and I had seen a year or two back—The Blue Brigade, some such name? I can't laugh, I thought, not on my husband's death-day. Then two men brought out a stretcher on which lay something concealed from head to foot in a red blanket, and all desire to laugh left me.

When I got back I saw that Etta had been acting postman. People we had scarcely spoken to drew back their curtains and stared brazenly; others pretended to be surprised to find no milk delivery, though it wasn't due for at least an hour. Etta met me in the hall; she was wearing a nylon fur hat pushed onto the back of her head. I couldn't have worn it at that angle, and nor could anyone I knew, but she achieved a kind of panache.

"Where do you suppose you're going?" I asked.

"I leave," retorted Etta defensively. "A house of death, it is not nice."

"It's not nice for me," I agreed, "and less nice still for Mr. Harding. You can't go yet, you'll have to answer some questions—oh, not mine . . ."

"The police?" she cried sharply.

"I wouldn't be surprised. Anyway, they'll want to talk to anyone who saw him last night."

25

"I can say nothing," Etta declared.

"Then that's what you'll have to tell them. Oh, and don't go off into any fine tales about him being poisoned by the hare, because that isn't what he died of. In the meantime," I went on, "you can get me some breakfast."

She looked outraged. "I cannot eat," she declared.

"Not your breakfast—mine," I pointed out. Anyone might think Derek had been her husband, the way she was carrying on.

She turned reluctantly toward the kitchen. "You wish I should make you an egg?"

I had a sudden vision of Selborne's *Second Book of Birds*: "The Etta-bird, a fur-crested specimen, lays its eggs scrambled."

"Yes," I told her, "you can make me an egg."

She'd removed the hat when she brought the eggs in; they were remarkably well done. I turned the keys in the locks of Derek's "den" and his bedroom to prevent her snooping, though what there was to snoop after, I couldn't be sure. She was inclined to languish a bit, as if it were bad form to do a fair day's work for a day's pay on such a morning, but I wasn't going to leave her on her own. For all I knew, she'd have dramatized herself into Derek's *femme fatale,* the woman he yearned for and couldn't get (though I'd never heard him utter a complimentary word about her), and being denied her favors, had found life not worth living.

The police wasted no time getting to work. They reminded me of moles that thwarted in one direction, start tunneling in another until they've reached the light. Naturally, they wanted to know about the tablets. I told them what I'd already told Dr. Tewkesbury.

"You could check with Dr. Fletcher," I said, "but I'm sure my husband hasn't had any tablets from him."

"Had you perhaps had any that he could have laid hands on?" they suggested.

"Oh, not for ages," I said.

"How long ago is ages?"

I thought. "Eighteen—twenty months—Dr. Fletcher might know—he warned me they might have side effects. The side effects were so unpleasant I threw the rest away at the end of a week. I never keep old prescriptions. I can't even remember what they were, or what a fatal dose would have been," I added.

"You've no objection to our checking that fact with your doctor, Mrs. Harding?"

"Eighteen months ago?" I said. "Would they still work?"

"It would depend what they were."

"Anyway, he wouldn't. It's not as though he had cancer or anything."

"He had no private worries that you know of?"

"He might have had some at work, I don't know, but that wouldn't worry him too much. It never has before, so why now?"

"He may have had some personal trouble you didn't know about."

I thought of Daisy and Daisy's successors. "Nothing that would drive him to those lengths," I said.

"Can you tell us the name of his employers, Mrs. Harding?"

I gave him the address. "I don't know the number, I never rang him there."

"You don't mind if we use your telephone?"

"Of course not. It might be more private upstairs." I remembered I'd left Derek's room locked. "I supposed you'd want to examine it," I said.

"You've no objection?"

"Why should I? But I shall be very surprised if you find anything that helps you."

"You say he came in late last night?"

"Not really late, about seven-thirty. We usually eat at seven on Etta's account. She likes to get off by eight."

"He said nothing at all unusual?"

"He said he'd had to see a man who might be useful to us both one of these days. It was worth a dried-up hare. We had hare for dinner last night," I explained.

"No name?"

"It wouldn't have rung a bell with me if he had. He never brought his business colleagues home, never spoke of them. He thought business should be left at the office at the end of the day."

The officer who had gone to telephone came back. "Mrs. Harding, were you aware that your husband had left his original firm some months ago?"

I stared. "Are you sure?"

"I spoke to Mr. Gully himself. You didn't know?"

I shook my head. I could see this was another bad mark against me. Wife doesn't even know about her husband's job, though I'd often heard other wives complain of their husbands' secrecy. "But what's he been doing ever since?" I cried.

"He had a temporary post with a firm selling stationers' accessories. On the sales side. It was for three months, and he was told yesterday that they weren't proposing to renew the contract."

So that might explain his air of exhaustion, defeat almost, and the two or three drinks he'd had before he got home. His man who might do us both a bit of good was a figment of his imagination. For the first time I wondered if he really had reached the end of his tether and had taken the stuff himself.

"You're quite sure," the policeman went on. "Incidentally, Mrs. Harding, you should be warned of your rights; you don't have to answer any of my questions without your lawyer being present, nothing you've said up to date could be used against you."

Big deal, I thought. I haven't told them anything to date. "I don't know any more of what happened than you do," I pointed out.

"But if you do choose to answer, then I have to inform you that your answers could be taken down and might be used in evidence."

I'd heard it so often in films and on the television screen, I didn't believe it when I heard the words addressed to me in my own house. "Why should you suppose I've anything to hide?" I demanded. "If I had any idea where he could have got the stuff, I'd tell you."

"I thought you told us that in no circumstances could you imagine your husband taking his own life."

"It's absolutely out of character," I admitted. "But I didn't know about his job when I said that. All the same, he'd never take such a final step unless there was some much graver reason. I mean, he wasn't afraid of starving, I've got a job, he'd expect another one to turn up. He—he wasn't in any trouble with this last firm?"

"His accounts were in excellent order. Naturally, we inquired. It's just that they didn't feel he was the man for the job. Spoke of getting someone younger."

Of course, I could see what he meant. Men of thirty-two shouldn't be feeling for the next rung of the ladder, they should be climbing confidently. How do you tell a policeman that your husband has no head for heights?

"As for the source of the tablets," the man went on carefully, "you assured us that you had barbiturates in your possession at one time."

"Eighteen months ago," I snapped, "and I threw them away at the end of the first week."

"Then can you explain how it is that Etta Cusack" (that was the name her family had adopted when they settled in England, the blunt-tongued English being unable to pronounce the original) "declares that she saw a phial of white tablets that could have been barbiturates in your medicine chest only a few days ago?"

"She can't have done and she must be crazy to tell you so. I don't think there are even any aspirin there. And whatever it was that Derek took, it wasn't aspirin."

The officer took out an envelope from which he shook a narrow plastic phial, the sort you get from chemists or hospitals.

"Might this have been the container?"

"I suppose so. Isn't there a date on the label?"

"The date seems to have been torn away."

"What else is written on it?"

"The capsules. One to be taken at night."

"If they'd come from a hospital they'd have had a name," I said. "Dr. Fletcher must know. I never went to anyone else. But there were no more pills in that phial a week ago than there are now."

"In that case, Mrs. Harding, why keep the phial?"

I hesitated. It's always hard to explain your own small meannesses. Some people can't bring themselves to put first-class postage even on a family letter, they buy the cheapest postcards and walk a mile to a market to save fourpence on a pound of tomatoes. My meanness is small containers; I never can bring myself to throw them away. I have a little plastic box with a bee painted on it that once held kirbi-grips, minute cardboard boxes that came with earrings or a scarf ring. They clutter the back of a drawer in my bedroom, but I can never quite bring myself to throw them out. I can't really have believed that phial would ever be any use, but I told myself, You never know, one day I might want something just like that. It's all akin to keeping bits of string and scraps of wrapping paper. But just try telling the police that.

"Are you sure you haven't misunderstood Etta?" I asked, a new facet of the situation striking me. Because why on earth should Etta have concocted such a story? I didn't suppose she liked me particularly, but she had no reason for wanting to make trouble for me. If she wanted to give the impression that Derek had taken his own life—why? Because she'd refused him her favors? The idea was so fantastic I barely stopped myself from laughing aloud. Derek had hardly exchanged a dozen words with the girl—well, you know what I mean. And what he had seen of her he hadn't liked. Besides, if he wanted anyone to fool about with, and he sometimes did, he'd at least have kept the mud off his own doorstep. No, that wasn't the answer. All the same, there must be some reason. Couldn't the bitch realize her statement was tantamount to accusing me of murder?

Murder!

I was aware of a heavy hand on the back of my neck. "Keep your head down, Mrs. Harding. Right down. The faintness will pass."

I hadn't even been aware I was going to faint. "You don't have to break my neck," I mumbled, struggling for freedom. It occurred to me that was one of the few things the State could no longer do for you. "If you believe this fantastic story of Etta's," I said, "ask her when I'm supposed to have given my husband the tablets? She was with me all the time in the kitchen, Derek opened and poured the wine, he helped himself to food, and Etta made and brought in the coffee. He sometimes had a whiskey-and-soda at night, but he stayed in his study, I don't know . . ."

"Miss Cusack says there was no dirty glass in the study and none in his bedroom."

"So?" I said.

"If you were mistaken and the tablets had not been destroyed, would it have been possible for your husband to get possession of them?"

"I didn't keep the medicine chest locked, there wasn't much in it, just burn ointment and dettol and disprin. My husband liked that when he had a headache, but I hadn't bought any lately."

"There are still some disprin tablets in a bottle in the medicine chest."

"What was Etta doing prying into the chest anyway?"

"She wanted a piece of elastoplast for a cut thumb."

"She knows all the answers, doesn't she?" I tried to remember if I'd seen a patch on her thumb during the past week, but I couldn't recall.

The police were putting another question. "Is it a fact that your husband had refused you a divorce recently?"

"Not all that recently."

"But you had asked him?"

"I suggested it once, it must have been two or three months ago, but he wouldn't hear of it. We never discussed it again."

"Is it a fact he said, 'Only over my dead body.' "

"He might have done," I allowed. "It's a very ordinary expression."

"Did you expect him to change his mind?"

"Not unless it suited his book. There was no one else he wanted to marry, I'm sure of that."

"And you, Mrs. Harding?"

"I might have wanted freedom to start a new life," I acknowledged. "We were getting nowhere fast. But I intended to start it on my own. And if," I added warmly, "you think that his refusal gave me a motive for wanting him out of the way, let me assure you you're wrong. I only had to walk out. I have an independent job, we have no children, and if later on I wanted to form fresh ties, the law's on my side, isn't it?"

"After five years."

"It would take me that long to decide to marry again. The burnt child and the fire—remember. Oh, don't get me wrong. My husband didn't ill-use me, he didn't drink (well, not to excess anyway), he wasn't unfaithful in any sense that mattered, but I felt I'd made the wrong choice and was young enough to start again."

I even wondered if Etta had said anything about Tom. I didn't intend to drag him in if he could be kept out. He was in the States, a newly married man no doubt; and I'd known about Rosamund, even Etta couldn't suggest him as a motive. I'd destroyed his few letters and the only one that might conceivably have compromised us had never been sent.

The police didn't leave a stone unturned. They even knew about the telephone call from Lucy Foster that Derek had taken, thus giving me a minute and a half alone in the dining room. I wanted to ask them if they thought I had the powder crunched up in a handkerchief ready to sprinkle on his dish of hare during his absence. But perhaps they'd believe I'd arranged for the telephone call. So far as I could see, Etta hadn't forgotten a thing.

They went at last, without asking me to accompany them, but telling me not to leave the district without warning them.

"How can I go?" I demanded. "I've got to attend the inquest." I asked them if they knew when it would be. They said I should be notified. When the door had shut I felt as though I'd been climbing a mountain without oxygen. I could have done with a slug of whiskey but I couldn't go into Derek's study where the bottle was kept.

Etta came marching in wearing the black fur hat. "I go," she announced dramatically. "I do not come back." She cast her latchkey on the table.

"I suppose you do know what perjury is," I said.

She flamed up at once. "What is this—perjury?"

"Giving false evidence on oath. You realize you'll have to repeat everything you've told the police in a court of law." I hoped it wasn't coming to that, but no harm putting it strongly now.

"I say only what I know," declared Etta.

"Then you've got an imagination a best-selling novelist might envy," I told her grimly. "All that stuff about seeing sleeping tablets in the medicine chest! If you saw anything, it was disprin in a bottle."

"They were not disprin and they were not in a bottle."

"How's the sore thumb?" I asked, and saw for once I'd caught her unprepared.

"The thumb?"

"The excuse you gave the police for meddling with the contents of my medicine chest."

"It is well," she said defiantly. "I am very healthy, but I am also careful."

"And intelligent. So tell me why I should want to poison my husband?"

"He say—a divorce only over my dead body." Then she stymied me by adding that the police had warned her she should not discuss the affair with anyone.

"Just remember it'll be your word against mine," I warned her.

"Why should I say what is not true?"

"That's what flummoxes me," I acknowledged.

She flounced out with no more heart than a winter lettuce. It was after I was alone—I couldn't even ring Lucy, because what could I say? She'd have said in her open fashion that no one could believe a bitch like Etta, only I wasn't so sure. After a while the loneliness of the house was more than I could bear. I remembered I hadn't said anything to my office, so I telephoned them. Derek suddenly, desperately ill—I told myself childishly that an inquest hadn't found him dead yet. They said to keep in touch, here's hoping. They'd be saying something quite different in twenty-four hours' time.

Eventually I went to the local Classic where they were showing *101 Dalmatians*. I had seen the film in Madrid with Derek, with Spanish dialogue that neither of us could translate. I chiefly remember the long queues of natives waiting to get in. I suppose I chose it now because there were so few people in it—you couldn't count the old witch. As I came out, refreshed because just for an hour or so I'd felt myself a member of the anonymous community, I heard someone call my name. It was a neighbor, one of those side-splitting spinsters who know their special vocation is to brighten up the world.

"So you're still allowed out without an escort," she said.

I staggered at the speed with which the story had spread. Still, ambulance, policemen, Etta, even the doctors I'd called and who hadn't come—it was a thousand to one against anything being kept secret. I got the idea Miss Ponsonby would be on my side even if she *knew* I'd poisoned Derek. Men! she'd say, with the humorous uplifted eyebrow of women who know nothing about them.

The telephone rang several times that night to reassure me I wasn't overlooked. I suppose, but after the second call I didn't answer it. Too many sick jokers, all out to have a thrill for sixpence. We're told to feel compassion for them, they can't help it, they're psychological misfits, but that night all my compassion was for myself. I didn't have time to grieve for Derek. At least he was out of it all.

I couldn't rest even in sleep. I found myself in an underwater cavern with the tide coming in, and every time I approached an exit to swim back to land, something appeared in the aperture and drove me back. And the sea came on and on. When I did wake the tears were pouring down my cheeks. I sat up, propping my eyelids open, fearful of falling asleep again and returning to the same hideous dream.

3

The inquest was a very brief affair. I identified my husband's body, the doctor certified cause of death, and then the police asked for an adjournment to enable them to pursue their inquiries. I heard someone say, "That means they're not satisfied it's a natural death. Got their beady eye on someone, I shouldn't wonder." Kind Lucy Foster met me outside the court and took me home for coffee, to the obvious disappointment of those who had gathered at The Kettle on the Hob in the hopes that we should be there, too. The verdict also meant that Derek could be buried. Nobody came to the funeral, although quite a number of people stood on the sidewalk to see the coffin being shoveled into the hearse. It seemed to me he was shoveled away rather than buried. None of his women turned up—well, that was hardly to be expected, he probably didn't recall the names of any but the last, but no one came from any of the firms he'd worked for, not even in a private capacity. He'd never put himself out to make friends among our neighbors, not worth it, he said, when he was away so much. He'd leave the poodle-faking to me. I drove unaccompanied to the cemetery in the single mourning coach. He didn't even have a lawyer close enough to attend. The vicar was a stranger—anyway, we weren't church people—and there were no funeral meats.

On my return the house felt cold and dusty. Etta didn't come back, the telephone rang once or twice. Then, a few

days later, turning the corner of the street, I saw there was a
police car at my gate. My instinct was to turn and run—but
where? There wasn't any place in the world that spelled safety
for me. I heard with mystification and dismay that the police
had brought a warrant for my arrest.

I said feebly, "You have to be joking." I couldn't have
said anything more out of line. They were accompanied by a
policewoman, and she came to watch me pack, I suppose to
make sure I didn't try to smuggle out a cutthroat razor or a
phial of deadly poison, though by that time they must have realized the house contained neither. Every window was agog
with faces as I came out and got into the police car. It was
quite a surprise not to find a fringe of sightseers standing round
the station door.

Next morning I was brought before the Magistrates'
Court and charged. I was remanded in custody; no question of
bail, of course. I was granted a certificate of legal aid, since all
the money in our account was in Derek's name. I pointed out
that I'd earned most of it, but that didn't help me. As an accused wife I couldn't touch my husband's estate.

The lawyer they sent me was called Dowler; he was a
pale, short man with dark hair and green eyes. He shook my
hand as if he were afraid he'd never wash off the guilty stain,
and I heard myself say, "Have you ever defended an accused
murderer before?"

He said, "I don't defend you, Mrs. Harding. I merely act
for you. Counsel for the accused defends you."

"Going on what you've told him?"

"To a large extent."

"Do I get counsel on my certificate?" I wondered. If so, I
didn't suppose I'd get any very big bug, whereas I'd heard that
in a poison case the attorney general himself represents the
Crown.

Mr. Dowler by-passed that. "Mrs. Harding, I must warn

you that if any of my questions should appear to you offensive, I am only asking those that are likely to be put to you in the witness box."

His first question floored me.

"Mrs. Harding, did you, in fact, poison your husband?"

"If I'd poisoned him I wouldn't be needing you or defending counsel," I pointed out when I'd got my breath back. "No, of course I didn't. I told the police . . ."

"Mrs. Harding, I must warn you your best course will be to answer the questions that are put to you as briefly as possible. No comment and, above all, no suggestion or criticism is desirable." Then he said, "As to your previous answer, if the Crown's contention were true, then you would need counsel more than ever."

"You mean, even if you knew I was guilty, you'd still go on trying to prove I was innocent?"

Mr. Dowler flushed darkly and said something about a crook.

"I didn't call you a crook," I demurred. "I just thought perhaps that was your job."

"I did not say *a* crook, Mrs. Harding. I should be sorry to think there was more than one. I was referring to a lawyer of that name, whose boast is that he only defends the innocent."

"You mean, he gets them off even if they are guilty?" I was amazed.

"According to him, his clients are never guilty."

I quite saw you'd never get a man like that on legal aid; his commitments must stretch on to the end of the seventies. I said as much.

Mr. Dowler stiffened. "I can assure you, Mrs. Harding, I shall do my utmost for you. Shall we proceed?"

He took me through my story point by point. I had been questioned so strenuously and so often by the police, the answers ripped out as though being drawn from a slot machine. I only seemed to start vividly awake when he spoke of Tom Cribbins.

"He doesn't come into this," I said sharply.

"The prosecution may consider that he does."

"But he was in America weeks and weeks before my husband died."

"It's a two-way trip to America, Mrs. Harding."

"Not for him. He'd got the job of his dreams, he found the girl of his dreams" (I supposed that was how he regarded Rosamund) "and I'm not sure I didn't hear they're married by now. Anyway, there was never any question of his marrying me, even if I'd been free."

"We must hope the prosecution won't attempt to make capital out of him. Of course, if they do, they are bound to warn us in advance."

(But they didn't. I was doubly thankful I hadn't sent that letter.) But I clung to my contention that in no circumstances would Derek have taken his own life. He was too much accustomed to other people picking up the pieces. Mr. Dowler looked uncomfortable, he didn't think I was going to make a very sympathetic witness.

Mr. Dowler switched to something else. "You are sure you have no notion of the identity of the man your husband was meeting that night?"

I shook my head. "He just said a man who might be some use to us. My first suspicion was that something had gone wrong with the job and he was hoping this man might offer him another opening."

"He wouldn't have told you?"

"He didn't even tell me he'd left the pharmaceutical people. What it boils down to," I went on, my temper rising, "is whether the jury believes me or Etta Cusack. I know it's a cliché that when one half of a married couple dies, the survivor is the police's first suspect. It makes things too easy for them."

"I trust you will refrain from making such observations in the witness box, Mrs. Harding. It hadn't occurred to you that unless the guilt of the surviving party has been proved in a large percentage of cases, the cliché would not exist."

The man talked like a dictionary. I longed for someone human. "If I'd intended to poison my husband, surely I'd have planned it less clumsily," I suggested.

"It is one of the mysteries of the profession how criminals who plan a quite ingenious crime allow themselves to be entangled by details that would be obvious to a child of ten."

On we went. Presently I asked him if he had anyone in his mind's eye for the defense. He said the question of counsel was foremost in his mind. "We have first to ascertain the probable date of the hearing, and then inquire into the list of Q.C.s who would be free and willing to accept the case. I have one or two names in mind who are not averse to taking a bit of a gamble."

I didn't ask who paid the bill. I wondered if there was some society to help the litigious poor, but I said nothing. I'd had enough for one day and I saw plenty of interviews ahead.

After he'd gone I sat thinking about the jury. Surely it was reasonable to suppose they'd be sympathetic to an unhappily married woman; but on the other hand, perhaps a kind of righteous jealousy would operate: I've put up with John, Susan, Arthur all these years, and in spite of temptation, have never tried to push him out of a window or her under a bus, so why should *she* get away with it? And if any of them had failed, you could be sure they'd be more set in the paths of righteousness than the others.

Two visits later Mr. Dowler announced, clearly surprised despite his unemphatic manner, that Mr. Aubrey Fielding, Q.C., had agreed to undertake the defense.

"We are extremely fortunate," said Mr. Dowler in the voice of a curate announcing Here endeth the First Lesson.

"He is definitely a rising man. In fact, he has already risen above many of his contemporaries."

"I wonder what he hopes is in it for Walter," I murmured, not pausing to consider my words. "Well, I shall be able to ask him, shan't I?"

"Counsel does not always consent to see a client before the trial," Mr. Dowler warned me.

"That sounds plain staring bonkers," I protested. "Why on earth not?"

"Because counsel must rely entirely on fact, he must not allow a personal prejudice in favor of his client to influence him."

"I never heard such rubbish," I exclaimed warmly. "I've got counsel for the prosecution and probably half the jury and two thirds of the people in court against me from the start. I need someone prejudiced in my favor."

I didn't ask what this Fielding creature was like; something gray and gnarled no doubt, which birds would mistake for a log if he sat cogitating in a wood. And on this, this spiny dinosaur, my whole future depended.

And so it did, but by no means as I had anticipated.

Mr. Fielding did come to see me, and he brought his junior counsel with him, a dark young man called Latimer, with a face like a Border terrier and with a terrier's controlled eagerness. Mr. Fielding was a man of average height, about thirty-five years old, with dark auburn hair brushed away from his face and cut close on the nape of his neck. Even before he had finished his first brief interrogation, I found myself wondering how Mr. Dowler, that faithful watchdog, had contrived to persuade this man to accept the case. He took me skillfully through my story, asking very few questions, then at the end he asked two or three that were quite unexpected.

"You told Mr. Dowler your husband said he had had to

see a man who might do you both a bit of good. You're quite sure he didn't mention a name?"

"No. He didn't. But if he had, it wouldn't have registered. I never met any of his business acquaintances. He never brought them home."

"Did you think he meant any particular man or was it just a *façon de parler?*"

"I think it's just a thing people say—had to meet a man about a dog . . ."

"Did you think it conceivably might be a woman?"

I was startled and showed it. "It never went through my head, but I suppose it could have been."

"Did he go around with women, so far as you knew?"

"Not when he was at home." What had we done when we were sleeping under the same roof? The first couple of years we'd gone out after the manner of young marrieds without ties, no invalid mother, no baby; later he'd watched television or gone across to the pub. Sometimes I went with him, sometimes not.

"But when he was away? He was away quite a bit during those four weeks when he was unemployed."

"I always thought he played around with girls when he was on his own, but nothing serious. He was one of those people who hate being alone."

"Does the name of Mrs. Ellen French mean anything to you?"

I didn't need to answer, he could see by my face that it didn't.

"From inquiries Mr. Dowler has been making," Mr. Fielding told me punctiliously, "we have reason to think that it may have meant something to your husband."

"You think she may be the one he saw that night?"

"Thinking won't be sufficient, Mrs. Harding, but if she admits to knowing your husband, that might be a step toward admitting that she saw him that night. In any case, he may

42

have confided something to her he hadn't told you; it very often happens when a man is in a bit of trouble, his wife's the last person to hear."

"You're not treating this as a romantic affair?" I exclaimed. "He wouldn't do anything desperate on any woman's account, he wouldn't need to. He could have had a divorce as soon as the law allowed. If he did take the pills himself, it wouldn't be on account of any woman." I thought a moment. "She hasn't come forward."

"She may not come into the picture at all. In fact, unless there is proof that she can help the case, naturally she won't be called."

I wondered about Derek and the unknown Mrs. French. He'd never mentioned her name—well, he'd never mentioned the names of any of the others—but had he been sleeping with her or under her roof, probably the same thing, during that blank period that so far wasn't accounted for? I realized, like a lot of other wives, I daresay, that after four years of marriage I knew practically nothing about my husband—I don't mean surface habits and turns of phrase, but the man himself. I found myself accused of the murder of a stranger.

I thought a lot about her after Mr. Fielding had departed. I didn't expect to see him again before the trial. Without making any promises, he had given me an impression of security, though I had to remind myself it could be a case of the house built on sand.

I thought the wardresses looked at me a bit oddly that night. They had been impersonally kind. I don't think it mattered to them whether I had poisoned my husband or not. They didn't behave as though I was beyond the pale, they showed no personal sympathy. To them I was just another silly bitch who'd landed herself in a jam, and now had to foot the bill.

What chiefly impressed me at the beginning of the trial

was the astonishing isolation of the prisoner at the bar. From various films and television series I'd always imagined defending counsel at the prisoner's elbow, and I believe in many of the American states this is the case. But my counsel didn't even sit near the dock. I watched his junior and wondered what he made of it. Just a case, I supposed, from which he must hope to learn something at the hands of the master. As for myself, I seemed to have been transformed overnight into The Prisoner.

When I was brought up, my glance wandered around the court. I recognized a few faces—it was almost a full house, I reflected: "These domestic crimes always pull 'em in," I'd heard one wardress mutter to the other—neighbors who'd thought it worthwhile to catch the early-morning train and battle with the commuters to be here on time. Everything about the scene was awe-inspiring. Derek and I used to laugh about old stuffed shirts in white wigs looking like the White Rabbit. We'd never appreciated the majesty, the aloofness of the law. The judge was even installed higher than anyone else. All come to question and ferret and accuse and defend one person; and the others, the virtuous and free, the unfound-out people, cramming the benches—with me behind a bar.

After counsel for the prosecution had been speaking for a short time, my bewilderment grew. Who was this woman who mysteriously bore my name and had been married to a man called Derek Harding, and was now on trial for his murder? She was a hard-featured calculating creature, wanting the best of both worlds, with friends she didn't share with her husband (Lucy Foster? surely not Tom Cribbins?) and a bed she wouldn't share with him either. I wanted to stand up and shout, "You're talking about the wrong person. I like a man in my bed as much as anyone; it's not my fault if he wanted a separate room" (but naturally, all the pillars of justice would think it was), "and anyway I never shared my bed with anyone else." But, of course, I did nothing. I remember Mr. Fielding saying, "You are in court solely to answer questions put to you

44

by myself and counsel for the prosecution, and naturally, His Lordship, should he see fit to put any. I shall know what points can be profitably raised and those it will be best to ignore."

So I sat tight and waited for Mr. Curtis to get his come-uppance when my counsel had his turn.

Etta was, of course, the prosecution's chief witness. She had been well coached, and stuck like glue to her story of seeing the tablets in the cupboard a day or two before Derek's death; sensibly, she couldn't be absolutely sure which day. Later she assured Mr. Fielding that no, it was not possible that she should have made a mistake and confused the disprin tablets with the deadly ones. The bottles were not the same, she said disdainfully. She told the court she had been aware for a long time, almost from the start, that it was not an harmonious household. Like a horse and a mare that pull in different directions, she said, and some people laughed.

Mr. Justice Innes turned as black as thunder. "Mr. Curtis, can you not keep your witness in order?"

Etta was quite untroubled. She said she knew the question of divorce had been raised. The deceased had been heard (by her) to say, "Over my dead body." She had heard the telephone ring during dinner that night and seen Mr. Harding come into the hall to answer it. He had been out of the room one and a half to two minutes. The prisoner had not left the dining room. She had found no used whiskey glass, as was normal in the study or the lounge (as she would call it), but that was no proof there hadn't been one or that it hadn't been washed.

Once again Mr. Justice Innes intervened. "The witness must understand that she is here to answer counsel's examination and later cross examination, not to advance theories. Perhaps," he added to Etta, "you are not conversant with the British legal system."

Etta glared. "I am honest," she declared. "I only say what is true."

"Your last comment can be construed as nothing but speculation," Mr. Innes told her sternly. "Pray continue, Mr. Curtis."

During this exchange I glanced at the two women members of the jury. For the first time I detected signs of sympathy in their sharp faces. I wondered if, perhaps, they had had *au pair* girls in their households, and so were inclined to take everything a foreigner said with a pinch of salt.

"Now, Miss Cusack," Mr. Curtis was saying, "you are quite sure there's no possibility of your confusing the two kinds of tablets in the medicine chest?"

"I am quite sure."

"You made a thorough inventory of the chest?"

"I do not understand what is inventory."

"You know what was in it?"

"There was these tablets and there was the disprin. Then presently there is only the disprin and the empty container."

"You were in the habit of going to the chest then?"

"I go for a piece of elastoplast. The chest is not locked."

Mr. Curtis raised the question of the divorce before he sat down. I suppose he wasn't so happy as he would have liked and as Etta appeared to be as the result of that last bit of examination.

Then it was Mr. Fielding's turn. I had listened, appalled, as the answers piled up like fagots on a bonfire, but he deflated her with no appearance of triumph or violence.

"Miss Cusack, you say you heard my client discuss the question of divorce with her husband?"

"He say over my dead body," returned Etta dramatically. "A few days later he is dead. What would you think?"

It had been more than "a few days," but Mr. Fielding proceeded to turn this misstatement to my advantage. "It is for me to ask the questions," he reminded her, "but since you ask, I should expect a guilty wife to wait rather longer before acting, particularly as she might have been overheard."

"She did not know I hear," cried Etta triumphantly. "I was outside."

"On the further side of the door? Then the jury may think you were mistaken in what you believe you may have heard."

"I come here because I am asked," cried Etta. "It is not nice to be confused with a murder."

"Until the jury has returned a verdict, there is no proof any murder has been committed. Now, about the medicine chest, Miss Cusack. You are certain you inspected it on two separate occasions?"

"I do not inspect. I go for a piece of plaster."

"And you see two containers with white tablets in them."

"That is what I have said."

"Then a day or two later you pay a second visit to the medicine chest. For more plaster?"

"The door swing ajar. I go to close it."

"And while you are closing it, you notice that one of the phials is empty?"

"I have said . . ."

"You also told the jury that the cupboard door is not kept locked?"

"That is so."

"So anyone in the household, even a stray visitor, could have helped him or herself to the tablets?"

"There is no one else in the house. There is no visitor. Only Mr. and Mrs. Harding and me." She saw in his eyes the question he hadn't asked. "I do not touch it," she declared.

"And Mrs. Harding declares she never even saw the pills. And you told my learned friend that Mr. Harding was not likely to take his own life."

"That man never kill himself," cried Etta scornfully. "He love himself too much."

I could hear Derek's voice saying, "You would think a

girl who had spent most of her life in this country could have learned to talk Queen's English by this time?"

The prosecution had one or two other witnesses, but no one of any real importance, and Mr. Curtis said the Crown rested its case.

4

Defending counsel opened his case when the court assembled next morning. I was Mr. Fielding's first witness. He had already warned me against expecting too much. "What we should both like," he said, "is for me to be able to *prove* your innocence, but the only way of doing that would be to produce the actual criminal. What we must look for is a verdict of Not Proven. That's not a verdict an English court can bring in, but it's the actual meaning of Not Guilty in a great number of cases." The other thing he said was, "I can't warn you of the actual way in which the prosecutor will shape his questions. More depends on this than you might realize, just as your replies will be weighed by the more intelligent members of the jury word by word." He quoted a case of that famous advocate, Marshall-Hall, where a verdict involving a life sentence was won by the change of emphasis on one particular word. "Be on your guard," he said. "This is your real testing time." I hoped I acquitted myself reasonably well before prosecution.

Mr. Curtis' questions were adroitly put, as you would expect, but Mr. Fielding had taken me over the ground and no new points were suddenly thrust before me. I told the court I had married for love (at that time I had no other motive for exchanging my free hopeful life for the more limited existence Derek would offer) but the marriage had gone sour, as the best-meant marriages could. We had never had a really violent disagreement, I had no intention of abandoning my husband, though I would have been glad of a divorce by consent; and I could offer no conceivable reason why Derek should take his own life. Nor could I suggest any way by which he could have obtained the means. I repeated my assertion about the pills I had thrown away, and insisted that I could think of no reason why Derek should have thought of taking his own life.

When I left the box Mr. Fielding put up a barman called Ted Upover, who served at the Cock & Fosters, a name I'd never heard in connection with a bar before. This man said he had known Derek by sight for about three months; he used to come in for a pint quite often in the evening. Sometimes he brought a lady with him, but more often, alone. He didn't seem to know many of the regulars, but he hadn't been coming more than three months. He'd heard the lady address him as Derek. No, he wouldn't like to swear to her identity on oath. On that last evening Derek had come in alone, looking rather distracted, soon after six-thirty. He had had two or three double whiskeys—not an unusual order, but it stuck in his mind because he'd always thought of Derek as a beer man. Just before he left he had said, "Love you and leave you. Shan't be round these parts after tonight. Got a new venoo."

"And did you deduce from that, Mr. Upover, that he was trying to convey any special message to you?"

I thought Mr. Curtis was going to rise and protest about leading the witness, but Upover said simply, "Well, I didn't know, did I? Chap who's been coming for a few weeks says he won't be coming again. Well, no skin off my nose. It's not as though he was one of the regulars."

That was a note that was to keep sounding right through the evidence. The next witness was the personnel officer in the stationer's firm that had given him his congé that last morning.

"Did he seem particularly distressed?"

"I wouldn't say distressed. He never seemed particularly anything. What I'd call the drifting type. Log comes down the river, he hangs on for a while, then the current swirls it away and he looks around for another log. No complaints of his work, except that he seemed a square peg in a round hole, not clubable, not really knowledgeable enough for the job. We like 'em to start younger," Mr. Chubb assured the court. "Once past thirty, they're set in their ways. Young chaps are climbing all the time, ready to learn all the new tricks." No, he'd never heard him utter what could be called a threat of self-destruction. When he was told the partners weren't going to renew the option, he'd laughed and said, "Well, that's that, isn't it? All that's left to me now is to chuck myself in the bloody river." But that was just a *façon de parler*. Lots of chaps talked that way. He, the witness, was dead sure Derek hadn't been serious.

That was really the trouble. None of them seemed to take him seriously; he filled a gap, the gap widened, he couldn't fill it any longer. It seemed like his epitaph.

Then Mr. Fielding proceeded to put the cat among the pigeons by calling Mrs. Ellen French.

The woman who came into the box was never likely to see forty again, but in her case, that didn't matter. She was very smartly got up, waved and manicured. She made me think of the centurion who said to his servants *Do this! Go hither!* and was instantly obeyed because he expected to be obeyed. You didn't have to look twice to know that her bag was real crocodile, not one of the clever new plastics, or wonder whether she did her own hair. I could quite see the attraction she would have for Derek. And he for her? Well, there was the famous charm, of course, and she was the sort of woman who likes to let the driver think he's holding the reins, whereas in fact she is manipulating every step of the journey. If he'd married a woman like that, I thought, either we'd have held an inquest on him at the end of the first six months, or never held an inquest at all.

She admitted that she'd known Derek for about four months. They'd met at someone's party—really, with the tiniest shrug that annoyed some of the jury, she couldn't remember whose. One went to so many. They'd become friendly when he started work in her neighborhood. He had formed the habit of dropping in, now and again they went to the local, or they might dine together. Until that last day she hadn't realized he was a married man. He'd never mentioned his wife or dropped the smallest hint about family connections. She thought it possible he was divorced, but they never discussed the subject. He had seemed rather unlike himself that last evening, jumpy was the word she used. She asked if something had gone wrong with the job, and he said well, that was only temporary anyway, he'd have been moving on in any case, but his wife was beginning to ask awkward questions, had even mooted a divorce.

"This came as a shock to me," said Mrs. French. "I got the impression that he was really fond of her but couldn't quite live up to her weight. 'When women run the universe,' he said, 'we'll all get short shrift.' I said, 'Well, do something for me. Don't mention my name.' And he said, 'Naturally not, but she wouldn't worry if I did. She knows she's got me for keeps.'"

Mr. Fielding was inclined to treat her as a hostile witness, pressing her on what seemed very small points. Under that pressure, she admitted that she'd lent him money, which, of course, hadn't been repaid.

"I will ask you this, Mrs. French. Did you expect the sum to be repaid?"

She bridled a bit at that. "I said a loan, didn't I?"

Mr. Fielding let that go. Then he said, "One more question, and please consider well before you answer. Is there any possibility whatsoever that Mr. Harding could have got the tablets on your premises, unknown to yourself? If, say, he went to the bathroom . . ."

She thought. "I can't remember if he did that particular night, but he knew where it was—naturally. Not that that would help him. I've never needed anything of the kind. I suppose," she volunteered, "he could have got them from some private source. Friends of mine tell me it's not difficult, if you don't want to ask your own doctor outright."

He'd seemed a bit down in the dumps; she supposed something had gone wrong with the job, or he was upset about his wife. She wouldn't have put him down as a suicidal type.

"I told him there's always tomorrow, and he had one for the road and he went off. I suppose," she added with a sudden stab of bitterness, "he couldn't keep his big mouth closed when he got back."

I felt a stab of pity for her. Hers wasn't a very enviable situation, a woman of the world, as she clearly was, ditched by a man who couldn't even hold down an inferior job. Some women, of course, enjoy inferior men. And now to have all her affairs made public—it's bad at twenty, it must be worse at forty. I wasn't quite sure I believed her when she said she didn't know Derek was married, but I was pretty sure she hadn't known we were still living together. It was a humiliating setup for one who clearly was accustomed to calling the tune.

Lucy Foster confirmed that she hadn't rung me up by arrangement, and anyway, she wouldn't have done so while a meal was likely to be in progress, but she knew Etta liked us to finish at seven-thirty. She and I had spoken of a rearrangement of our upholstery class; she hardly knew Derek at all.

I don't think she got much attention. People were working out in their minds the effect of Mrs. French's evidence. They must have appreciated the slant my counsel was trying to put over, though he was walking a tightrope. There wasn't a grain of evidence against her—there never had been a grain— but she was a one-in-a-thousand possibility, and that might be just enough to swing the scales.

When finally the judge summed up to the jury, I thought he leaned very slightly in my favor, but that might be my imagination. Certainly he didn't attempt to soft-pedal any of the evidence—he had a good word for the witnesses, who, he said, had done everything possible to ease the jury's task, but he did remind them that justice is as ill-served if the guilty went free as if the innocent were wrongfully condemned.

The jury went to consider their verdict, shepherded by an officer of the court. The judge vanished, people started moving, I went downstairs to wait.

The jury was out for what seemed to me a long time.

"Longer they are, the better for you," one of the wardresses assured me. "Drink this, dear, you'll feel better."

I sipped the strong sweet tea, realizing that whether I was found innocent or guilty, it was all one to them. Once I heard that the jury had come back to ask for advice, as they couldn't entirely agree among themselves. Those were the days of the unanimous verdict. He'll tell them to take their time and try and come to an agreement, nodded Wardress A to Wardress B. Well, they don't want to spend all this time for nothing.

After an hour and thirty-five minutes the jury returned. I stumbled up the stairs, with an odd feeling that my hands were bound behind my back. The court had filled up like milk being poured into a jug. I looked around but didn't see the face I was looking for, but I wasn't seeing very well. Then the foreman of the jury answered the clerk of the court. Not guilty, he said. I felt as if a great bubble had blown up in my face. The jury was looking a bit sheepish, even the two women didn't send me a congratulatory glance. Somebody said, "Let the prisoner be discharged," and a wardress touched me on the shoulder. But I shrugged her hand away, I wasn't under her jurisdiction any more. I was searching the court frantically for a sight of my counsel, but he wasn't there—unbelievably, he wasn't there.

"If you're going to faint, dear, you can't do it in court," one of the wardresses muttered. Already people were staring. I could visualize their thoughts. She's had a shock, never expected to make it, that's what they were saying. I turned and went out of sight. I had imagined a glorious sense of relief and excitement if the verdict went my way, and I'd never allowed myself to think anything else, but all I knew was a sense of the most terrific anticlimax.

"I suppose I go home now," I said dully.

The little gimlet-eyed wardress said, "No one coming to fetch you, dear?"

"Well," I said brazenly, "I couldn't make any arrangements, could I? I didn't know . . ."

"Haven't you got a friend or family, someone in court?" But the only family I'd had for years was already underground. I just prevented myself saying so. "Then I'd wait just a little," the wardress went on. "Don't you agree, Nelly?"

Nelly did. "Why should I wait?" I demanded mulishly. "I've as much right as anyone to go where I please when I please."

"They'll soon tire of waiting," Nelly assured me comfortably.

"What are they waiting for? Surely not to see *me*? They've been doing that for days."

"It won't be just the ones who were in court," the gimlet-eyed one explained. "You can't really blame them, life's a bit monotonous these days . . ."

"So it's a kick, a bit of a giggle really, to get a ringside view of someone who might have been sent down for twenty years. Or are they waiting to spit in my face?"

Before the women could register disapproval, steps sounded outside and young Mr. Latimer came in, rather breathless, as if he was afraid he'd lost the race.

"I'm glad to have caught you, Mrs. Harding," he said. "Mr. Fielding asked me to say how sorry he was he couldn't stop for the verdict, though he had no doubt what it would be . . ."

I goggled at him, filled with a less than reasonable dismay
—chagrin, rage, I'm not certain which.

"You mean, he *left the court?*"

"He had an urgent message about his father, he had a
stroke recently, and things had taken a turn for the worse. Mr.
Fielding is the only son, and he felt he must go to Grimsby at
once. He'd done everything he possibly could for you."

"Supposing they'd found me guilty?" I asked.

"Mr. Fielding never considered the possibility, but if that
had occurred, naturally we should have lodged an appeal."

"Well," I said, picking up my bag, "I'm sorry not to have
the opportunity of thanking him for all he's done for me. But I
daresay I could write to his London address."

"I am sure a letter would be forwarded," agreed the Border terrier courteously.

But of course that meant someone else would have read it.
Already I could convince myself he barely remembered my
name. "I may as well go home now," I continued brightly.

"Streets are still pretty crowded," offered Mr. Latimer.
"I'd give it a little longer, Mrs. Harding."

It was like the echo of a conversation I'd heard before.

"Where are you proposing to go?" my terrier went on.

"Home. Where else?"

"That's a pity." I thought when his turn came he'd be
quite an imposing figure, too. "Is there nowhere else?"

"Why should I be driven out of my own home?" I demanded. "Anyway, I'd be even more of a cynosure in an hotel.
Besides, there's my job."

He looked doubtful. "Aren't you proposing to take a little
holiday before you go back to work?"

"Waste a little more time, you mean?"

"I'm thinking of the press," said Mr. Latimer. "There are
always a few sensation hawks hovering around after a case like
this. It won't last. Someone will hijack a plane, or a Cabinet
Minister will commit suicide, and that'll distract public atten-

56

tion. It's just for the next few days, three or four, say . . . I'm only passing on the advice Mr. Fielding would have given you," he added sincerely. "Still, if you must go back, at least let me see you home, I've got my car. And when you get in, take the telephone off its hook and don't answer any bells, unless you're certain it's a real friend on the other side of the door. And if you find any anonymous letters in your box, destroy them unopened."

He told me to pull up my scarf, duck my head when we reached the house, and give him the latchkey so he could get the door open. In the car I remembered that I hadn't said good-bye to the wardresses, but I think I already belonged to their past.

There was a small crowd waiting expectantly on the pavement opposite my house. Curtains were drawn back discreetly. I felt, illogically, more furious with Derek than I'd ever been in my life. To subject me to this! Did they expect me to have grown two heads or be openly branded with the mark of Cain?

Mr. Latimer got out of the car and walked up to the nearest group as belligerently as though he were proposing to drop a smoke bomb among them. "What's happened?" he demanded. "Been an accident? Why hasn't someone called the police? There's a phone box on the corner."

They were so taken aback that a number of them started to oil away. I even heard one woman mutter, "Dessay that's the chap. No wonder she didn't want to bring him into court."

My companion opened the front door and I dashed in under cover of his arm. Though there was still a good deal of daylight left, he went around drawing the curtains. As he came back through the hall, the telephone started to ring. Before I could prevent him, he had jerked it off the hook. He listened for a minute, then said, "You should see a doctor before someone turns you in." He banged down the receiver to cut the connection, then lifted it and laid it on the table. "A lot of freaks will try and get through," he warned me. "Half of them won't be more than ninepence in the shilling. But it won't last. All the same, if you get the chance of moving for a week, don't hesitate. A trip abroad would be fine, and the name of Margaret Harding won't register across the channel."

"Really," I exploded, "there should be clubs for women like me—Madeleine Smith, Lizzie Borden (yes, I know they're both officially dead, but in one sense they'll never die). And there was that woman in York—Ogilvie, was that her name? And Madame Whosit of Rouen. Oh, I should think we could number quite a healthy subscription list."

I knew I was talking nonsense, but I couldn't stop. After Mr. Latimer had gone, I wondered about the trip abroad. But I should have to produce a passport, name, photograph, standing (widow—self-made?) and wherever I went, someone would recognize me, because that's the way life likes it to be.

The doorbell rang several times that evening. Twice soft voices called, "It's a friend, dear, a friend." But I knew I hadn't any friends left, and I wouldn't be deceived. Much later I opened the door a crack to reassure myself the normal world still existed, and I saw that one of the voices must have spoken the truth. There was a pile of provisions on the step. Bread. Butter. Half a cooked chicken. Milk in a bottle. Suddenly I was hungry. Only when I'd got them all back to the kitchen did I see the note pinned to the bird's breast: *At least this isn't poisoned.*

I threw it out of the back door in a wide sweep, and the black and white cat from No. 27 came out and fought for it with the marauding tom who lived on the car park. But I ate the bread and butter and drank the milk, because they were all I had, and they were all in their original packagings. I tried to make myself believe that the Border terrier was right when he declared that by next week people would forget about me. But faith was losing out that night.

Next morning brought a polite note of congratulation

from Willis' and a check for a month's pay. Like Mr. Latimer, they were sure I would be the better for a trip abroad, would feel more able to make arrangements when I'd had a rest. Nothing was said about hoping to see me later, and there was no reference to a certificate of character. For all they minded, I could get swept out to sea with the rest of the flotsam and jetsam.

5

I wrote to Mr. Fielding at his office, and a prim acknowledgment came back, saying he was still out of London but my letter would be shown to him on his return. After a few more days I got tired of rushing to look at the letter box when the postman called, and put the house in the hands of agents. I took back my maiden name by Deed Poll, becoming Mrs. Margaret Cooper. I couldn't revert to my unmarried status, because my ring finger gave me away. Besides, I still felt married, or rather, I didn't feel like a spinster. Which was reasonable, as I wasn't one. I left London and found myself a flat in Salisbury, which has a cathedral that is an inspiration even to the unbelieving and is a splendid center for starting out to anywhere. Perhaps the twentieth century would produce its Salisbury pilgrims.

I'd been in Salisbury a few days when I got a letter forwarded from London. It was Mr. Fielding's long-delayed reply. He explained about his father (who had since died, involving the son in a lot of legal footwork) and reminded me that the longer and, he was sure, the better part of my life still lay ahead. One day perhaps we might meet in happier circumstances. He sent me his kind regards.

In Salisbury, I got myself a job working in a bookshop. In the evenings I planned a novel based on my own experiences. There were to be three main characters: a man who died not from natural causes, and two women, suspicions being evenly distributed between them. I decided to write the story from the point of view of Ellen French, the second woman, who hadn't been accused. I thought a lot about her just then. I suppose it's true to say her intervention, though not voluntary, really saved my life, or saved me from life imprisonment. If she was absolutely innocent of Derek's death, she'd had a pretty raw deal. She must have hoped I'd be found guilty, it was the only way she could hope to be exonerated. I wondered if there'd been any repercussions for her. She'd said she never had sleeping pills, but she also let out that there were under-the-counter ways of getting them, which didn't sound too difficult. I supposed we should never know the truth. If she'd really been in love with Derek and realized he'd been leading her up the garden—well, if I had to choose between her and an infuriated lioness, I'd pick the lioness. I mulled over all this for some weeks. Then it occurred to me I wasn't making much use of the life Mr. Fielding had got back for me, so I tore up my emotional ms. and wrote some short articles for a local paper and then some (better-paid) for a women's magazine.

I used to think about the future in a vague kind of way. Would I marry again? I was only twenty-three, and the thought of living like a spinster for the rest of my life seemed hilarious rather than depressing. I never thought I might share a house with another woman, not for another thirty years or so anyway—and what was I going to do in between? I wanted what I'd always wanted—a home, a background, a husband, a dear companion, children. I wasn't afraid of work, I enjoyed fresh contacts. But what would a prospective second husband think when he heard about the first? I couldn't hope to marry him and keep my past a secret. And how would that past affect our children? But I didn't brood overlong on these specula-tions. I was busy, I was happy in my work, I was free. I created a social life for myself, made new friends, joined an art class, took holidays to Greece and Rome. I was planning a cruise that would take me to Jerusalem when Mr. Fielding fulfilled his hope that one day we might meet again in happier circumstances.

The bell rang when I was working one early spring evening, doing my weekly book column for the provincial paper, with the wireless playing low to drown disturbing sounds outside—cars going by, people calling from upper windows, dogs barking, car radios bawling. I'd lost my fear of opening to an unexpected call, but after a number of local houses had been broken into, I'd put a chain on the door of my top-floor flat, and after dusk I always kept it on. I used to lean out of the window at night and try to make out the figure waiting on the step below. I did this tonight, but all I could see was a rather broad-brimmed black hat (that had, I thought, a vaguely ecclesiastical tilt), which didn't help my identity problem at all. Missioners of a dozen creeds were liable to turn up in quite extraordinary gear, from prim Lutheran to modern hippie; and there were the charity collectors and representatives of strange political sects.

The bell rang again, commandingly, as though whoever pushed it knew I was there. There were people going up and down the street, as there always were at this hour; I wasn't melodramatic enough to imagine a gun in my ribs. I was thinking more of the book I was reading for review than about my unknown visitor. I was remembering my editor bidding me remember that books are written for the multitude, not the individual. The individual outlook is a luxury, he said, and luxuries are strictly for millionaires. The story had a Finnish background . . .

I still had Finland in mind when I opened the door.

I stood in a daze. I'd endured shocks before—the morning I found Derek dead, that other morning when I came back to find a police car outside my gate. But this was a shock of a different nature. I knew now why, against all common sense, I had kept his letter for over a year: *I hope one day we may meet in happier circumstances* . . .

I must have invited him in, because a minute or so later we were climbing the endless stairs—nothing so modern as a lift in this building. I remembered how visitors would pose Christina Rossetti's question: Does the road wind uphill all the way? He didn't ask that, he only said in a quite untroubled voice, "What a good naturalist you'd make." And when I stopped to stare, he went on, "You go to earth as completely as a partridge, that bird that can transform itself into a part of the landscape, so that you could set your foot on it before realizing it was there."

I said, feeling like a disembodied spirit, "It seemed a good thing to change my name."

"So long as you realize that doesn't change you," he agreed. "How many times a day do you do these stairs?"

"Oh, you get used to them," I said vaguely. "You get used to anything. Even to being a person without a past."

I wondered if he could conceive what it was like, behaving as though life had started only eighteen months ago.

He stopped dead on the last flight. "My dear girl, you're talking nonsense. No past indeed! Why, you carry it round with you like a hump on your back. Because you don't look in the glass, you may pretend it isn't there, but that doesn't prevent other people seeing it. Accept yourself, Margaret, unless you propose to spend the rest of your days anticipating a miracle."

It was miracle enough for me that he should be there, that he should call me by my name. It might be an accident, but surely it showed how—how intimately he thought of me. My heart thudded fit to burst. I thought I might drop down in a faint. Margaret Harding had married a man called Derek; now they were both dead, let them rest in their grave. But when I tried to explain this, he said, "How very unfortunate! It was

Margaret Harding I came to see. I never met Margaret Cooper."

We had reached the top floor at last. I pushed open the door of my flat. I thought my place had never seemed so welcoming or so warm, no wonder I didn't mind about the stairs. I offered him, first a chair, then a drink. I switched on another lamp, and the reflections from the gold shade painted the ceiling. I drew the curtains, gold brocade on old wooden rings, bought second-hand in the Monday market.

"How true it is you take your world with you," he said, rejecting the chair and walking around the room. It's something I always long to do myself in a new environment. I had a Canaletto, the one where everyone wears fancy dress and the Grand Lagoon is blocked with gondolas, and a lovely print of a dark red camellia. Beauty unadorned.

"I wonder where you find your dramatic—no, your non-dramatic—world," he said. "No past, no terrors, no griefs—no happiness either, I suppose. It may be safe but it sounds rather a Sleepy Hollow to me."

I brought him a dry martini. "It suits me very well," I said. (Only was it going to be enough now, after this?) "It's a refuge . . ."

"Refuges are for refugees. You can't expect to stay one of those all your life. You've made a charming retreat here, but you're no bee to live in its solitary cell till its work is done and it dies. You mustn't imagine I make a point of following up my clients," he went on. "In fact, this has never happened before. A lawyer regards his clients much as a doctor regards his patients, people of infinite importance so long as he can serve them. But if he loses them or even loses sight of them, he doesn't take it as a personal loss. He's done his best, and as the old proverb says, an angel can do no more. But when you find your thoughts turning—and returning—to one particular person and that person no longer a client, then you have a problem on your hands."

"But when—I mean—when did you start . . . ?"

"Oh, I think from that first day I knew we were bound to meet again. I knew at all events I should never forget you, though presumably I could learn to live without you. It happens like lightning, or polio—you're struck before you realize you're in danger, and afterwards it's too late."

I nodded. I knew what he meant by being struck by lightning. I had to say something, however stupid; and it was pretty stupid. "You waited a long time."

"I had to give you a chance to reorientate yourself. You might not have changed but your environment had, and you had to get used to that. I didn't want you to spend the rest of your life wondering if you'd been rescued—you have to do your own rescuing. Now we meet as equals, no gratitude on either side, no hanging on because you're still lame and need a crutch. It's not a crutch I want, but a wife. Women too often marry for a background, but not you. You have your own background, that you created through your own effort. I am simply asking you to enlarge it to include me."

If I hadn't secretly loved him before, I would have loved him then. It was as different a courtship from my whirlwind romance with Derek as I could conceive. I knew it was true that even without him I wouldn't fall by the wayside, but what a barren road I should tread. And I knew, too, he meant it when he said he wasn't asking me to marry him out of compassion. I remember years later, appearing in a notorious divorce action, which he seldom did, he told me, "That marriage never had a chance. He married her out of pity, and though compassion is a great virtue, it's no foundation for an enduring relationship. Pity's like a gold crown; the wearer may be proud of it, but sooner or later the sheer weight of the thing presses him into the earth."

Aubrey and I were married very quietly in Paris two months later in front of the mayor. I daresay the gossip writers put two and two together and had a field day, but we didn't care, because we didn't know. He took me to Venice and Florence, and so by road to Assisi. "Austria can wait for another year," he said. "I don't want you to find yourself in the position of a client I had whose husband crammed their honeymoon so full of high art that she was provoked into saying, 'Henry, if I see one more painting of a saint, I shall declare myself a pagan and that would be enough to annul our marriage.'"

"She sounds fun," I murmured.

"Her husband still thinks so," Aubrey agreed. "That was ten years ago."

I found myself hoping he'd still find me fun ten years hence.

And now the ten years were up. We'd had Gavin at the end of the first year, but the baby daughter we both welcomed so ardently only lived a few days and there'd never been any more. There was the terrible time when Gavin was four and our doctor diagnosed spinal meningitis and suggested a visit to a specialist. Dr. Rowbottom took tests and told us to wait. It was only four or five days, but that time took on the nature of eternity. Clocks didn't move, life was static. Then after the period of anguish came the verdict that the diagnosis had been a faulty one and our little boy would live. It was the worst scare of my life, worse than standing trial for Derek's murder, because in my heart I couldn't believe innocence would not triumph, even before Aubrey's intervention. But in the face of Gavin's illness I was helpless. Aubrey, I thought, was more fortunate than I, since he had his work—at all events, he went to his chambers during the interminable day. He turned down a plum of a case on the Western circuit, because we couldn't bear the thought of being apart at that time. Then we heard the good news, and I took Gavin to Devonshire and Aubrey stayed in London, coming down when he could.

Since then fortune had smiled on us. Aubrey had prospered, Gavin had grown tall and strong, I was happier than I'd dreamed it was possible for anyone to be. And now, when the glass seemed Set Fair and Aubrey's name was being openly mentioned in connection with the birthday honors, out of a clear sky—this! A cheap envelope, a common postcard in an anonymous illiterate hand. I found myself back where I had started, back to the same question—why? After so long—why? Aubrey was away for about three days, probably my correspondent knew this. But didn't he know, couldn't he guess, that Aubrey was also our banker, that without him I wasn't much better equipped to meet a blackmail demand than the proverbial church mouse? So—why not tackle him? Only, if X knew so much, he must also know you'd get blood out of a stone before you'd get a penny of blackmail out of my husband.

I picked the disgusting thing up in my fingertips, realizing as I did so that this was a very melodramatic thing to do. One thing seemed obvious, the writer must come from the past. What fresh "evidence" could be dredged up now I couldn't conceive. Everything that had happened on that fatal night had been torn to shreds and laid out on the public block. And like the caterpillar that improves with keeping, whatever my correspondent had unearthed, or believed he had unearthed, had been growing in value. I made up my mind that this was something I would deal with by myself. I was a woman of thirty-three, I must stand on my own feet. Inevitably, my thought went back to Tom Cribbins. I hadn't spent much time thinking about him in the past ten years. I had heard he was married, with two sons, but on his visits to Europe he never attempted to get in touch. Now I might meet him in the street and not even recognize him.

My first obvious step was to keep the appointment and learn a bit more about my enemy. I looked at the card again: . . . BE AT THE TEAPOT AND DORMOUSE AT 6 P.M. TOMORROW NIGHT.

For the first time I looked at the postmark. The card had come from the Charing Cross district and had been posted the previous day. Which meant that the appointment was for tonight, not, as I'd been thinking, for tomorrow. I looked at my watch, pushed the postcard into my handbag and went upstairs to prepare for the rendezvous.

I'd no notion where or even what the Teapot and Dormouse was. It sounded more like a teashop than a public house, but surely a rendezvous at a teashop would have been fixed for an earlier hour. I got down the telephone directory. The only Teapot and Dormouse I could find (and was it likely there would be more than one?) was near Euston Station. I knew that part of London a little, had been once or twice to the airport there and walked through the gloomy back streets. Probably that was where the Dormouse lived.

I set out rather early, since the street was one I didn't recognize by name and I felt this was the kind of meeting where it would be a mistake to arrive late. I put on a very plain black suit, with a black and gold scarf over my head, and flat-heeled black shoes. Nothing noticeable, I decided, nothing to make a local say, "Wonder what *she's* doing here."

I traveled by bus and subway; even a taxi might be noticeable there; I didn't know how far Edgeways Street was from the station. I found it fairly easily in a nest of small dark streets all running into one another. The Dormouse was a biggish sleazy-looking pub flanked by one of those faceless hotels with names like Balmoral or Buckingham where strangers slip in and out as anonymously as houseflies. The signboard showed a dormouse peering into an open teapot. The lid was poised above his head, and just out of sight I could visualize a strong red hand intent on thrusting him into the dark. There were two bars, saloon and public, but I thought if X wanted any privacy, it might be better to carry on our conversation in the saloon bar.

The only barrier that separated the two was a wooden

partition reaching as far as the bar counter. The barman served both bars, moving easily from one to the other. I imagined the place paid its way chiefly on account of the air terminal, though I was to learn it had its regulars. The saloon bar boasted a few tables against the wall, most of them at this hour of the day unoccupied. I seated myself at one of them. For the first time I began to wonder how I was to recognize my enemy. But presumably the writer of the card hadn't worried about that, taking for granted that he would recognize me. The minutes ticked on. I had come too early for my appointment. I hadn't been sitting long before the barman, who had time on his hands, came round to ask negligently what I was drinking. I started to say I was waiting for a friend, but that might have invited the comeback "Stood you up, has he, dear? What a shame!" and perhaps a pert reminder that this was a bar, not a station waiting room. So I said quickly I'd have a glass of dry sherry.

The barman, as I feared, was a bit of a wag. "You see he pays for it, dear," he said, bringing me a glass of something that tasted like liquid brown sugar. I sipped it wryly. I had to make it last till X appeared. If he hadn't come when the glass was finished, I'd go home and tell myself I'd been made a fool of. But I wouldn't believe it. Even the worst jokes aren't usually as bad as that. More people came in; there was quite a lot of noise from the public bar. Very few of the newcomers seemed to recognize one another, and there was none of that verbal to-ing and fro-ing Aubrey always enjoys so in a pub.

A voice said suddenly, "This'll do us," and I looked up to see a man and a woman preparing to occupy the vacant chairs at my table. I began to say I was sorry, but I was expecting someone to join me, when the woman said, "This marriage seems to be suiting you all right. You've hardly changed at all."

For a minute I stared. I saw a sallow dark-eyed woman, putting on a bit of weight; the voice told me nothing. It was no more accented than that of my Mrs. Day. Then it came to me, and I wondered why I hadn't thought of her at once. Who else could it have been?

"Etta!" I said. "Etta Cusack!" She'd done her best to harm me ten years ago. What could she hope to do now?

"Mrs. Porter," Etta corrected. "Meet Gerald—Mr. Porter."

She sat down as comfortably as though the saloon bar was her own living room—I remembered how she'd always insisted on calling it a lounge.

"Hi there!" said Gerald.

He was a tough-looking little man with no features to speak of, you could see him forty times and not recognize him the forty-first. His sort came off the assembly lines like pairs of shoes. His only distinguishing feature—it wasn't till later that it occurred to me he only wore it to make certain he *was* recognized on occasions—was an old-fashioned watch chain, the kind that used to be called an Albert, stretching across his waistcoat. A little gold fish charm dangled from one of the links. A ridiculous saying from my schooldays came into my head: Father's in the pigsty, you can tell him by his hat. And a new fear fell on me, because this seemed to suggest experience. He'd hardly be wearing it because he fancied it. Queen Victoria's consort may have popularized them and given them his name, but nowadays men wore watches on their wrists or carried folding ones in their pockets. I remembered being told once that a hand grenade doesn't look so very different from a child's toy till you pull out the pin.

"What's that you're drinking, Mrs. Fielding?" Etta asked briskly.

I pulled myself together. "If I said it was sherry I'd perjure myself."

"Better get her a gin-and-tonic, Gerald," Etta commanded. "Vodka for me. And mind it all comes out of the bottle and none of it from the tap. You'd be surprised what tricks some of these publicans get up to," she added, smoothing off her gloves.

"Have you worked in a hotel?" I asked. Something had happened to replace her original sullenness and suspicion with that commanding air.

"Well, you could say so. I didn't stop on after the trial," she went on. "Too many people pointing and talking. I saw this ad in a posh country hotel. Chambermaid. It wasn't what I was looking for, but you have to give the dust time to settle. The fellow who interviewed me thought Etta was short for Henrietta, and that suited my book. In a murder trial it's not just the guilty person who pays the bill."

"Particularly when you can't put a name to him or her," I agreed.

"Oh, I wouldn't go that far," Etta said. (Wherever she'd been, it had taught her to drop her foreign accent altogether. Or perhaps Gerald had helped.) "The police seemed pretty sure and, of course, I knew."

"You want to be careful," I warned her. "There's a law of slander."

"But you're not going to get up and repeat what I've just said to anyone, are you?" Etta asked, sounding surprised. "And there's no witness. I wonder what's happened to Gerald. Perhaps they had to send down to the cellar to get the vodka."

"I'm still waiting to hear why you suggested the meeting at all," I said. I saw her trick. She wasn't going to come into the open until she had her husband as a witness on her side.

"Came like a bird, though, didn't you?" Etta chuckled. "Mind you, you were wise. If the police had known as much about a certain person who'd gone to America as I did, the verdict might have been very different," she went on cozily. "I've always wanted to know—oh, here's Gerald coming at last— how much you told your husband. Of course, he was your counsel then . . ."

Gerald arrived, his hands laden with bottles. When he handed me my gin-and-tonic my hand shook so I had to put the glass down again.

"All set?" asked Gerald in a sort of cockney-sparrow voice.

"I was saying to Mrs. Fielding that if the jury had known as much about her and Tom Cribbins as we do, they might have thought twice about their verdict."

"I hope they thought more than twice," I said sharply. "And there was nothing about Tom Cribbins for them to know."

"They mightn't agree if they'd seen the letter you wrote him."

"The letter?" I stared. "Any letter I wrote to him went to America . . ."

Etta opened her bag and drew out a largish manilla envelope. From this she took something that looked like a photograph of an ancient inscription. "Perhaps you've forgotten." She grinned.

"It's a photostat," I said.

"You wouldn't expect me to bring the original, but don't think I haven't got it. That's the final piece of evidence referred to on the card."

I nearly laughed. "You must be crazy," I said. "A letter that was never sent."

"Well, we don't know that, do we? You wouldn't send the draft, of course."

"It's what's called a catharsis," I told her, not quite sure if that was the word I meant. "I never intended to send it. Tom Cribbins would assure you he never set eyes on it."

"Well, that's what you'd expect, isn't it? Only—how many people would believe him?"

"He had gone to America weeks before my husband died. He's married, with children—quite likely he's forgotten my name. We were never more than friends."

"That's not what the letter says. Colors get toned down in the mind with the years. Have another look at it, Mrs. Fielding."

I took the thing automatically and started reading the first paragraph. The next minute the blood poured into my face. Surely I'd never dropped so low. The melodramatic phrases joggled before my eyes. "He will never give me a divorce. I see no way out. I can't endure this half-life much longer, I keep thinking of the contrast with yours, so rich and free . . . I wish sometimes we lived in the Middle Ages when magic could be invoked."

I couldn't read any more. I put the card down. "Any comment?" asked Etta mockingly.

"It's just a hysterical outburst from someone who feels she's touched rock bottom," I said as composedly as I could.

"Others might say it was a desperate appeal from an unhappy wife to her lover."

"Tom Cribbins was never my lover."

"You'd be bound to say that, of course."

"If you were so sure of the importance of this—this . . ."

"Hysterical outburst . . ."

"Why didn't you show it to the police?"

Etta shrugged. "The police! One shows them nothing unless one is a fool."

"You know perfectly well you didn't show it to them because they'd have laughed in your face. You could never have brought a thing like that into court."

"Counsel for the prosecution then?"

"Didn't want to be tagged as a hostile witness," offered Gerald, joining in the conversation for the first time.

"Why not? She was hostile, no one could doubt that."

"I answered the questions I was asked. They explained to me there is a thing called contempt of court—"

"So why keep it all these years? The time to use it, the

very last time, was when I married again. Only, of course, you didn't hear about that in time to put in your claim."

"Wise people keep a nest egg. Each year, if they are sensible, it becomes a little larger. Presently the time comes for hatching."

"Not necessarily," I reminded her. "Sometimes it addles."

"Not Etta's eggs," said Gerald. "They wouldn't dare."

I picked up my glass—my hands seemed enormous—and took a swallow of the gin-and-tonic. It tasted like train oil.

"And if I tell you I'm not interested—what then?"

"You have the first offer. If not, there are others."

"You couldn't put a thing like that on the open market," I exclaimed.

"There is a series about to open in the *Morning Star*. It deals with unsolved murder mysteries. Gerald has seen some of the manuscript. He's a free-lance—the press, you know. Evidence that never saw the light. Oh, they're clever those people, they don't put their heads into nooses. But then, if it is so innocent, you won't mind."

"You wouldn't dare," I said, but I could hear the note of wobbling mistrust in my own voice. And then I realized that of course there was no question of their selling it to anyone except me. It wasn't just myself, it was Aubrey and Gavin. The question Etta had asked—how much Aubrey had really known about my relations with Tom—would be asked over and over again. And I had to admit that it did read like a desperate cry from an abandoned lover. And not long afterward Derek had died.

"Where have you been that you've learned so much?" I burst out.

"I have been working," Etta said.

"As a chambermaid, you told me."

"That was just for a start. I didn't mean to spend my life being a servant at everyone's beck and call. I looked about and saw the kind of salaries secretaries got, so I learned shorthand and typing and I answered an advertisement from another hotel even more posh than the Royal Marmaduke—in the West Country, that is, a very nice Regency building—and I was taken on as resident secretary. They get a lot of business-men staying there, come down for conferences and so forth, or think of buying an estate and want to get to know the neigh-borhood. It might surprise you, Mrs. Fielding— You're not drinking and it's time for second halves—anyway, Gerald, you can bring them . . ." He went off, cheerfully obedient, like a little brown dog, I thought. "Yes, as I was saying, they'll let a secretary know things they wouldn't dream of mentioning to their wives or sisters. Not human, see? Having computers won't make any difference to them. I stayed there awhile, then I got married, and I never went back to work. That is, after a while, not having a family, I started my own business. Type-writing mostly, authors' mss. a specialty. You'd be surprised how much money there is in it, Mrs. Fielding."

I thought I was past being surprised by anything Etta could tell me. Ten years had changed her out of all knowledge, giving her an assurance I could envy.

"Mind you, most of the stuff is trash, but it pleases the writers—time on their hands, I suppose— And talk about fussy—one woman even asked for two spaces between each word. I've got one or two names that would surprise you—personal recommendation, you know—and I keep my card in the stationer's window, people sometimes drop in with quite short jobs, but you know what they say—even little fish are sweet. I've got a one-room apartment round the corner, very handy. Of course, we don't live there—we've got a nice flat in Regents Park, one of that new block near the Zoological Gar-dens. We can hear the lions roar some nights, and Gerald goes to the window and roars back. He's so lifelike—there's a lot more to Gerald than appears on the surface, you know." (I supposed there had to be, or with her unscrupulous enterprise, she wouldn't have married him.) Etta began to laugh. "One of our neighbors wrote to the managers that someone was keeping a lion on the premises. Nothing said in the lease about not keeping a lion, I told her."

"You haven't explained yet why you dragged me up here," I said. "What do you hope to get out of it?"

"Here you come," said Etta over her shoulder, and patient Gerald brought a second supply of drinks. "Well, fact is, Gerald and I think of going to the States. I've been meaning to go for years now, but I couldn't go as the poor relation, could I? And we mean to go for good."

"And you're busy collecting the price of the fare?" I suggested nastily. I started to pull on my gloves. "What had you in mind?" I added in what I hoped sounded a negligent tone.

The figure Etta put on that wretched bit of paper was so astronomical that I looked a second time to make sure she wasn't joking. She wasn't.

"How do you suppose I could lay my hands on that sort of money?" I demanded.

"You ask her what a husband's for," Gerald suggested.

"If I were to breathe a word of this to Aubrey, you'd never see a penny, probably find yourselves in the dock," I flashed. "Blackmail . . ."

"What have you been saying to her?" Gerald asked. "I never heard a word about blackmail." No, I thought, that's why she sent you off to get the drinks.

"Of course," he went on, "if you've got a letter or something—but you never did, did you, Et?"

Etta must be an old hand at the game, I thought. She wasn't taking any chances. A postcard that couldn't be identified, sent from a seething London post office, no witness when it came down to brass tacks. Oh, she had me on toast. How could I possibly tell Aubrey about this? He trusted me, he loved me, but suppose he'd seen that crazy scrawl before his feelings had a chance to deepen, might they not have been like the seed that fell on stony ground and withered away from lack of moisture?

"Shall we say the day after tomorrow?" suggested Etta, reading me like a child's primer. "That'll give you thirty-six hours to raise the money."

"I've warned you, if I were prepared to accept your terms, I couldn't raise anything like that sum."

Etta nodded comprehendingly. "Just see what you can do, Mrs. Fielding. We don't want to be too hard, do we, Gerald? We all make mistakes. And there was that old woman who killed the goose that laid the golden eggs. Six-thirty suit you? The address is 14 Klondyke Street, it's only a stone's throw from here. That's why I suggested the Dormouse. It's not much of a place, but handy, and then you'd never see anybody you know here, and that's important, too. Bring a brief-case with you, if you're nervous of being seen stopping in Klondyke Street. Quite a number do, even if there's nothing inside but the evening paper. Gives the situation a professional air."

"Are you proposing to carry on your work in America?" I asked.

"I'm going mainly to get knit up with all my relations who've been over there for years. Mind you, we've kept up all the time. They'll be sort of a background for us, and a background's useful."

I wondered if that was why she'd married Gerald. "Have you been married long?" I asked, though I didn't really care.

"Three years since I met up with Gerald. Well, you don't much like being on your own. You found that, didn't you?"

6

We parted outside the Dormouse. They turned toward the main street; I saw them hail a taxi and get in. So they weren't going to the Klondyke Street office, but presumably straight home to Regents Park. I tried to picture Gerald deceiving a lion. He seemed more like a mouse, but you have to remember the feats with which mice have been credited—there was once a lion a mouse set free by eating through the tethering rope. It only went to show you couldn't be too careful. I didn't even look for a taxi. I went back the way I had come, by subway and bus.

Before I went to bed that night I turned out my jewel box. I had a few really nice pieces Aubrey had given me; I didn't intend to part with those to help fill a blackmailer's stocking. Anyway, he'd want to know what had happened to them, and I couldn't pretend they were being cleaned. I found a brooch my aunt had given me when I married Derek, a hideous thing I thought it, Brazilian diamonds in an antique gold setting. I'd read recently that Victoriana was coming in again. I might get something for that, though Brazilian diamonds don't rate very high. And there was a ring that had belonged to my mother, her engagement ring, small diamonds enclosing a not particularly ambitious ruby. Still, the stone was good quality, and so far as I could see, unflawed. And there was a solid-gold dog collar that had belonged to my grandmother. It was very heavy and in hot weather it clung to the skin, turning it green wherever the chain touched it. I wondered if that meant it was inferior-quality gold. In any case, costume jewelry was lighter and on the whole much better-looking. I found one or two other small bits and pieces and then got out my bankbook. I'd opened the account before my marriage and Aubrey had insisted I should keep it separately. There wasn't a lot in it, but everything was a help. I'd have to leave the account open, of course—it never occurred to me I might try and borrow money to satisfy Etta's demand. Why should I involve Aubrey in debt on her account?

Next morning I went down to Brighton. I didn't want to offer the stuff locally, for the trivial reason that like all other neighbors, ours are usually on the alert, and I might actually be seen offering jewelry, *sub rosa,* as it were, while my husband was away. For what reason? To pay gambling debts? To pay blackmail? It was too near the bone. There was a jeweler in Brighton to whom I used to go with my Aunt Helen. I didn't even know if the shop survived, and certainly the personnel would be different, but I remembered Aunt Helen saying that if everyone was as honest as Mr. Wincott, we shouldn't want a police force.

I decided to revert to my one-time name—pseudonym, if you like—of Mrs. Cooper. I recalled an address when I first came to London, Ambrose Gardens, Earls Court, and I might make use of that. I didn't really believe any jeweler would think pieces of such very average quality could be part of a haul, but I wanted to protect myself as far as possible at every point. It was a lovely day, the wind blowing off the Downs and the usual magpie crowd drinking coffee in the Lanes. I moved through them and made for the Arcade, where Mr. Wincott's name still flourished over the shop front, though naturally the shortish elderly man who came to meet me could have been any stranger. His interest decreased notably when he understood I had come to sell rather than to buy; naturally he wanted to make the least of what I had to offer. Still, he named a figure which, if smaller than I had hoped—who doesn't look for a miracle on occasions like these?—was nevertheless about as good as I could reasonably anticipate. It was the Victorian Brazilian diamond brooch that appealed to him most.

For form's sake I tried to persuade him to put up his figure, but he was like a little stone bulldog. I held up the dog collar, and he shook his head—very old-fashioned, very little demand for that sort of thing, he'd as lief have bought the other things without that—but I insisted they must all go in one lot.

"Might have it on my hands for some time before I find a buyer," he explained. "Meantime I'm out of pocket."

"I should have thought this kind of business was always speculative," I retorted crisply. "But it's the speculators who make the fortunes."

"Where they don't go bankrupt first," he said.

The total wasn't anything near the sum Etta was demanding, but I thought she had sufficient sense to realize this was the best offer she was likely to get. The letter wouldn't be worth anything to anyone else, and she might be asked some awkward questions, such as why hadn't she produced it ten years before, and if she didn't think it important then, why should she think it so valuable now? Of course, in those days I'd only been the Widow Harding, with next month's rent in hand and not much more. Now I was the wife of a prominent man. There was a world of difference.

I spent next morning writing a letter to Aubrey—I was never sure if he found time to read them when he was wrapped up in a case, did he even remember he had a home?—and went to the bank to draw as much money as I dared. Fortunately I had a lunch date, and my companion was so entertaining I was able, so to speak, to keep my sense of desperation at arm's length. Afterward I wrote to Gavin, who might well be feeling a bit homesick in the strange new world of school.

Klondyke Street proved to be a narrow side street turning off a main street behind Euston Station. Etta's apartment was on the ground floor of a tall narrow house, one of a row that gave the impression that people had stopped actually living there years before. Only lights in windows here and there and the sound of faint footfalls on the pavement convinced me I was still in a living world. The only bright spot was a lighted shop window at the farther end of the street, kept by an elderly woman selling tobacco and sweets and the cheaper women's papers. I had stopped to ask if she knew where Klondyke Street was and she had stared. "You're in it now," she said. She looked at me suspiciously, as if she thought I was trying to be funny at her expense. She was the only person I had spoken to since I left home.

There were five bells and the ground-floor one was labeled Cusack. So she'd stuck to her unmarried name—but why not? If you run your own business, it's probably an advantage not to use your husband's. I was just going to press this bell when the front door was flung violently open and a tall dark man with a black smudge of mustache and a wild Don Quixotish air, not noble and serene, but the look the old illustrators gave the Don when he was charging windmills, nearly bowled me over. I saw that he carried a black briefcase under one arm. I carried a file under mine; I had no briefcase and had no intention of buying one for this solitary occasion.

"Looking for someone?" he barked.

It went through my mind he could be a criminal flying from the scene of the crime. "Mrs. Cusack," I murmured, and he said ground floor and went tearing down the steps as though the bears were after him.

Etta was taking no more chances than she must. Besides the automatic porter, she had a device fitted to the inner door that enabled her to see the identity of her visitor while herself remaining invisible. She had been expecting me—I don't suppose it ever went through her mind that I might dodge the appointment—for she pressed the porter, and I came into a gloomy hall where an old-fashioned glass shade obscured a weakly bulb.

The inner door opened and Etta said, "Come in," adding that she had another appointment just before seven so we might as well get down to business at once.

"Do you like living in the dark?" I asked. I love light myself, but this room had only a desk lamp switched on, though there was an adjustable standing lamp by a table that held her typewriter and some folders. A radio crooned from somewhere.

"Everyone's life isn't as open as yours," returned Etta dryly. "We're not all so fond of the bright lights. Naturally, in our home things are different."

But I couldn't believe that leopards change their spots so easily. For this room was as dark and gloomy as the secrets it doubtless concealed. A dark flock wallpaper that had probably been there for a generation, chocolate-brown paint, long brown unpatterned curtains and another curtain that looked like green plush with a tarnished gold line in it hung on the wall behind the desk. I couldn't see anything admirable anywhere, except a rather nice brass candlestick of Cupid design. I thought at once, Aubrey would like that. I wondered if she kept it for use when dealing with clients whose business was so dubious it couldn't take a more powerful light. It didn't seem like Etta to have anything there simply for decoration.

"So you found your way," commented Etta. "I thought you would. Well, did you bring it?" Her manner made it clear she had no time for the niceties of conversation.

"I warned you I couldn't meet your demand or anything like it," I returned as coolly as I was able. "And I very much doubt whether you would do so well if you took your goods to some other market."

I had put a little purse on the table and now gave it a slight push in her direction. She picked it up and opened it. The house was eerily quiet. I wondered if all the other flats were unoccupied at this hour. It was the sort of place where anything, no matter how melodramatic, might happen.

82

"Are you alone here?" I heard myself ask. "Are you never afraid?"

Etta seemed genuinely surprised. "Of what? Of violence? It would take a good deal more courage than most of my clients possess to try to murder me."

"There's always a first time," I warned her. "And blackmail's a very dangerous profession. My husband says that where the murderer has normally only one enemy, every visitor you receive is your enemy. It must be like living in a snake pit. You may think they're all rendered harmless by having their poisonous fangs extracted, but fangs aren't their only weapons." I thought of those great snakes like boa constrictors who can deprive a victim of the last gasp of his breath.

"Gerald always has a list of my visitors, and I let them know it," Etta assured me. "Besides, I see to it that I can defend myself."

"Karate?" I asked.

"Being married to a famous lawyer has given you some very strange ideas."

Her hand had been lying in her lap under the table edge. Now she brought it out in a lightning movement; the desk lamp gleamed on something bright. Wicked and bright. I stared, unbelieving. "It's—is it a flick knife?" I asked.

She was laughing openly. "Have you never seen one before?"

"Never. Except on films, of course."

"Naturally, I only keep it for self-defense." Etta's voice was cat-cream smooth. "Every man is allowed to defend his own life with any weapons at his disposal. That was the mistake you made. You couldn't plead you poisoned your husband in self-defense."

"I didn't plead that I poisoned him at all," I pointed out.

"Does your husband know the truth?" she asked curiously.

"My husband established the truth."

"Nothing of the kind. You got off scot-free, but you weren't proved innocent. It was clever of him to drag that French woman into the case—a sort of red herring, don't you say?—but there was never any proof that she had a hand in his death."

"And no proof that I did."

"I tell you, I saw . . ."

"Your unsupported word can't be regarded as proof. I was unfortunate . . ."

Her eyes suddenly rounded like two great dark holes. "Unfortunate? You?" Her voice was black with bitterness. "What do you think would have happened if you had been in my shoes? If someone had come forward to say I had had barbiturates during the past year? Should I have been believed if I said I had taken them all myself or thrown away what were left? I, a foreigner—a servant? Oh, I should have been the perfect scapegoat."

While she was talking she seemed to shed the new smooth personality she had acquired, and returned to the sullen skin she had worn when she worked for us. I was too numb to speak. So here was the answer I'd been seeking for ten years. I knew now why she had made her statement to the police. Someone must be shown to have been in possession of the poison, someone who might deflect possible suspicion from Etta, who also had similar tablets. It explained such a lot. She had suspected everyone in those days, believed every man was her enemy. She hadn't concocted her story about me out of personal animosity, but to ensure her own safety. I didn't suppose she'd seen anything in the situation but that elusive safety. I didn't think then that she had anything to do with Derek's death; I didn't see that she had the shadow of a motive. He'd never made a pass at her, he'd never even liked her, she couldn't pretend she was compromised by him in any way, but she was convinced that the only person who could defend Etta Cusack was Etta Cusack.

"It was clever of your husband to put that Mrs. French on the stand," Etta continued, "but do you really suppose she killed your husband? If that were so, she would have taken a second dose herself."

"Perhaps she didn't have enough for two," I said gracelessly. "Make up your mind if you're going to accept my offer. If not, I'll take my money and go."

She had opened the purse and laid the money on the table. I watched her, and I knew she was going to take it. And soon, soon, she'd be in New York, and I could forget about her—at last.

She was fingering the notes doubtfully. "It's not very much."

"It's all I can raise," I assured her.

She looked up. "Those earrings you're wearing—they would be worth something."

I had loosened my scarf when I came into the room, and it had fallen back on my shoulders. The earrings in question were my favorites. I always wore them when Aubrey was away, for he had not only given them to me, he had designed them himself. They were little platinum shells with a diamond set in each. As Etta's curious eyes inspected them, I put my hands over my ears as if I couldn't even bear to let her look.

"They'd be no use to you," I assured her. "They're unique, made specially to my husband's order. No honest jeweler would take them without asking questions, and a dishonest one would be tracked down by the police at once."

"Perhaps you would not report the loss to the police."

"I shouldn't have any choice. Aubrey would notice I wasn't wearing them, and he'd know I wouldn't sell them."

Etta shrugged. "Anyway, they are too small for my ears. Then I will take what you have brought. Now I show you the letter."

There was a characterless picture of a seascape on the wall, and as I had half suspected, this concealed the safe. Etta turned to open it. Her flick knife lay open on the table. The banal drone from the radio made the air seem stale. It seemed to swell, though she hadn't touched it, and suddenly I felt I could bear it no longer. Taking her completely by surprise, I plunged past the edge of her desk and pushed back the shabby green curtain. The radio was clearly on a shelf or table behind it.

Etta, taken completely by surprise, turned white with anger, but not, I think, with fear. "Get back," she shouted as if she were ordering an unruly dog. "Stay the other side of the table."

But I hardly heard her. I realized now the significance of the radio music. On a table behind the curtain stood a tape recorder whirring gently away. The radio and the beating of my own heart would have drowned the noise it made.

I knew an anger then greater, I think, than any anger I had ever experienced before, greater than any I had felt toward anyone at the time of my trial. The force of that rage seemed to float me from the floor. I saw Etta's wild infuriated face, her eyes fixed on the knife that was just out of range. Clearly she had anticipated no violence from me. Out came my hand, stealthy and pitiless as one of those snakes I had had in mind only a few minutes before, and closed around that beautiful candlestick. Why should it be here? I had wondered. But now I knew. Oh yes, I knew now. I lifted it from the mantelshelf and swung it above my head.

"Put that down!" screamed Etta. "Do you hear me? Put that down."

And put it down I did, though not quite in the way she had intended. That tape recorder was almost as damaging as the evidence Etta kept stored in this horrible room. She might part with her "evidence" for a consideration, but the human voice endures, and doubtless she had guided the conversation along the lines that would best suit her. I tried to remember what we had said, but the words whirled in my brain like a cloud of gnats. Down, down came the candlestick, there was a crash and then another; the wireless died with a hideous scream, but I couldn't stop. I remembered Aubrey telling me once that when violence has a man or woman in its possession, the possessed will go on striking, blow after blow, though the essential object is attained. I saw my hand rising and falling, yet it seemed to have no especial connection with myself. It was an individual channel of power—I watched, helpless, fascinated.

Suddenly the fury left me; I trembled as if with cold. Etta faced me, the paper in her hand, the safe doors swinging. Her flick knife was just out of reach on the table. She lunged toward me, but her foot, catching in the cord of the telephone, brought it and her crashing to the ground. I remember thinking, Well, that won't be much use to you for the next two or three days. The instrument had cracked as it fell. With it had gone something else, like a small dark toad. This also broke open in its fall and I saw it was Etta's handbag. A passport came sliding out and I caught sight of an airline ticket. So she had told the truth about going abroad at all events. Perhaps, after all, she had made England too hot to hold her. I'd never believed much in her story of long-lost relations.

Money was spilling in every direction. Etta stooped and snatched at the purse and its contents. I came around the other side of the desk, surprised to find I still had the candlestick in my hand. The paper fluttered in Etta's fingers, and taking advantage of her stooping attitude, I leaned forward and snatched it from her hand. I thought for one instant she might get to work with her knife, but common sense told me not even she would know how to explain away a corpse on her premises. I set down the candlestick and stumbled out.

My hands were shaking so I could scarcely open the door into the street. There didn't seem many people about, and I told myself the sooner I got away from this district the better. Standing on the top step, I opened by bag as if to reassure myself that I'd brought my latchkey. Two Pakistanis strolled by on the opposite pavement, carrying suitcases. I supposed they had just come from the air terminal. A bus drew up in the main road and a man alighted. Just opposite the house a newsvendor had set up his stand. The man threw down a coin and picked up a paper, and I shrank still further into the shadows, because suddenly I was convinced it was Gerald. Still, he didn't look in my direction but vanished down the alley at whose mouth the newsstand was situated. It seemed to me the house must be empty or I should have disturbed someone with the hullabaloo I'd made.

I pulled on my gloves, retied my scarf. Then a girl came around the corner of the street, young, elegant, cool. I couldn't see her face under the brim of the fashionable hat she wore, but her shoes were Miss Rayne and she went by like someone in a dream. She didn't even look in my direction. Going to meet a lover perhaps. And young! I loved my husband, but I would never again wear that look of absorbed youth. Her passing even seemed to lighten the drab air. She went over the little crossing where I had crossed not half an hour before, and I watched her vanish into the little tobacco shop—it was scarcely larger than a booth. I looked up and down the road—no one in sight.

Now, I thought, hoping my legs would carry me. Now.

No lights burned, no head appeared at a window, no hand opened a gate. On the pavement, I turned away from the main street where the buses ran that would take me into the safety area. The dark was what I craved—to be invisible, move like a shadow out of this nightmare world back to reality. I realized I was still clutching the fatal paper whose existence had brought me here tonight. I turned sharply around the first corner, and stood in an ill-lighted byway, tearing the letter feverishly into scraps. I pushed some into a litter bin strapped to a lamppost; other scraps went down a drain. I thought someone was talking to me, but I think I was only talking to myself. A footstep turned the corner, and in panic, thinking it must be Gerald, I turned again and found myself practically face to face with the Teapot and Dormouse. It wasn't much of a refuge, but I didn't think Gerald would follow me here. There's safety in numbers, says the old proverb. I pushed open the door and went in.

At this hour of the evening business was brisk. It was what, I think, is known as a commuters' pub. Men leaving the day's work dropped in for a quick pint. Later perhaps, in the public bar at least, it would assume a homelier appearance. A dart board? Men drinking together at tables? I couldn't imagine the temperature ever warming much into something familiar and welcoming. Not a clubable place. I pushed my way to the bar and ordered a double brandy. The barman set it on the counter with a mutter as to price. He took my money, made change, never even looked at my face. I saw there were other women here, though no one else completely on her own. I carried the brandy away, drained it quickly, feeling a new false courage spring up in me as it ran warmingly through me.

The two or three people in the street were all coming toward the Dormouse; they pushed past, scarcely even acknowledging my existence. I walked a few steps, then heard a police car siren, and my heart jumped as violently as nearly eight years ago I first felt Gavin move within me. It wasn't there on my account, I told myself, of course it wasn't. These streets doubtless heard it every night of the week. A car with a flashing blue light on top went past two streets away.

I walked on, turning another corner when I reached it until I had to confess I was absolutely lost. For all I knew, I was walking in a circle. I didn't want to find myself near Etta's house again . . . The road I was on seemed endless and grew progressively darker. Occasionally a light flashed in a window, but no one spoke. I remembered dark ways in Dockland, with lights hanging from corners of buildings, and the perpetual invisible rustle. Rats perhaps!

Every step was taking me further and further from home.

Out of a patch of black shadow I heard a laugh, then the shadow deepened and moved.

"Meeting anyone, dearie?" a man asked with a kind of slurred chuckle in his throat.

I swerved as though I'd actually felt a hand on my shoulder, and almost tripped into the gutter. Twenty steps further on, a café bar, windows brightly lighted, was like a star in a black world. As I had fled panic-stricken into the Dormouse, so now I fled panic-stricken into this refuge. It was about two thirds full, a clean bright place with a few empty Chianti bottles hanging from the ceiling, though the café itself had no license. I thanked my stars it wouldn't matter how late I got home, since Aubrey was still in Liverpool.

At the counter I bought a cup of coffee and a sandwich and found a place at an empty table. I glanced around; no one could conceivably recognize me here. It was a complete cross section of the community—clerks, packers, students, lorry drivers, women cleaners, all very brisk and talkative, most of them smoking. They drank coffee and ate Danish pastries at the uncovered tables near the door, or ordered bangers-and-mash and spaghetti and chips at the tables further back that were covered with plastic cloths. The place smelled of food, but not of greasy food. The coffee was good and strong, the sandwich excellent. I drew a deep breath and unfastened the scarf so that it fell around my shoulders.

A jolly colored woman, with a little boy of about eight, came to sit at my table. She was carrying a bunch of flowers as bright as herself. Instinctively I smiled at the sight of them. Broadly she smiled back. "Nice—yes?" she said. "My sister, she grows them on a little balcony of her flat. Just to imagine. To grow all that on one little balcony."

The boy pulled impatiently at her sleeve, whispering something in urgent tones. His mother laughed. "You and your Coke!" she said, and she gave him some money and he danced away to the counter.

"You got one like that at home?" she asked me, and I said mine had just gone to school. She nodded her sympathy. "They grow," she said. "Soon they know more than their own folks, put you in the wrong."

The boy came back with his bottle of Coke and a straw and a packet of crisps.

"Lady lost an earring," he announced cheerfully as he sat down.

His mother rebuked him. "Maybe the lady only wear one earring."

But my hands had flown instinctively to my ears. It was true, one platinum shell was missing. I shook out my scarf, looked on the floor and the adjoining chair, but there was no trace. I hadn't expected there to be. I should have heard it fall.

"Maybe you leave one at home," proffered the colored woman.

But I knew that wasn't so. I remembered how I'd clapped my hands to my ears in Etta's room, and they'd both been in place then. If I confessed to Aubrey that one was missing, he'd say sensibly it wasn't the end of the world, he could get a duplicate made. But in order to claim the quite considerable insurance, I should have to report the loss to the police and answer questions as to where I could conceivably have lost it. Well, one thing was certain, I couldn't say I'd been visiting in this part of London. I could manufacture a story and no one could contradict me, but suppose the earring was in Etta's room and someone found it, as someone would be bound to do? I had tied my scarf as soon as I came away—would I have noticed a missing earring then? Most likely not, in the state I was in. I wondered if I could keep up a deceit with Aubrey—it must have slipped off in the street, I could say, only he'd had a special safety device put on, and he must have heard me say a score of times that they never slipped. And it would involve lying to the police, I supposed. It shouldn't be difficult to keep my movements dark, Aubrey would never dream of my visiting in these dank streets.

I remembered a story I'd once read where a man had been found guilty of some crime because he'd pushed a bus ticket into his pocket and forgotten about it. I turned out my bag to make sure I hadn't made a similar mistake. There was the possibility I'd dropped it in the Teapot and Dormouse, but I couldn't go back there tonight. In any case, it was improbable it would be found till the cleaner got to work next day, and common sense insisted it was even more improbable in such an environment that the finder would turn it over to the police. I thought I'd go around there next morning. It would be simpler to telephone, but that would involve leaving a name and number. I hadn't lost it on public transport, which left only Etta's apartment. One thing, if that's where it was, I could abandon any hope of its being returned by registered or any other post.

Leaving the café, I forged ahead and soon heard the sound of traffic. A quick turn brought me into the main street, and there were the great red London buses lighting the evening. An empty taxi went by and I longed to hail it, but already I had convinced myself that no one must ever know about the tryst I'd kept in these streets, and though it was, as they say, all Lombard Street to a china orange against any taxi driver remembering an individual fare, I thought the chips were piled heavily enough against me without my increasing the stack. So I let it go by and walked to the nearest bus stop—I didn't know the whereabouts of the nearest subway station and was too exhausted to inquire. Half a dozen people were waiting in a slight drizzle that had just begun to fall. None of them noticed me and in a few minutes a bus came up that took me to Piccadilly Circus. Here I got a taxi and was swiftly driven home. Even in the darkness the little garden seemed bright with the promise of spring, and as I thought this, I realized there were lights in the windows. I was still fumbling for my latchkey when the front door opened and there was my husband on the step.

7

I stared at him, scarcely able to accept his presence in the flesh. I felt as though the events of the past hour or so must be written large on my face.

"The return of Cinderella," murmured my husband. "Glad you came back in your pumpkin coach."

It was a joke between us that in fine weather if a bus would bring me near home, I would economically vote for the bus. Far better a taxi now than extra flowers on your coffin, Aubrey would urge, but I had become so used to comparative poverty that a taxi in fine weather still smacked to me of indulgence.

All the same, I was glad he had referred to it. In my fluster I could have told him I had been to the local cinema, where they were reviving a season of Greta Garbo films, and even as unsuspecting a husband as Aubrey would find it hard to believe that I should take a taxi for so short a distance, or indeed that the driver would consent to bring me. So I told him I had been to the Piccadilly Odeon. Fortunately, on the day of his departure—and separations from him made me feel like Shelley's widow bird mourning for her mate—I had actually seen the picture and I remembered the film in great detail.

"How was it?" he asked.

"Harrowing," I told him. No nudity, no four-letter words, just the theme that the hells of Faustus and Dante were altogether inadequate, and that the real thing might be condemnation to the eternal company of mindless evil. Those grinning, imbecile faces, the coarse schoolboy tricks, the humiliation of the damned, the absence of all hope of escape—oh, it made the little imps with pitchforks and the hissing serpents seem like a peasant's nightmare. In a way, it was fortunate for me; it went a long way toward explaining my obvious distress.

"Come and have a drink," Aubrey offered. "Take off your scarf."

But I knew the instant I did that he would notice the missing earring, so I made the excuse that I must change my shoes. In my room I found an alternative pair of earrings, also a present from Aubrey, little gilt Victorian griffons, changed my shoes and combed my hair.

As I came in, Aubrey handed me a glass. "Just what the doctor ordered," he said. "I rang twice to let you know I'd be back. I didn't know you were having a traumatic experience at a cinema."

"But why so early?" I asked. "Not that I'm not delighted to see you, of course. But I thought you weren't due till tomorrow night."

"I know now the feeling of doctors whose patients don't survive because they have insufficient faith in their advisers."

"You mean your client has thrown in the sponge?" With Aubrey to defend him? The notion was fantastic.

"In the most convincing way. He hanged himself. Don't ask me how these things are allowed to happen, it only bolsters up my conviction that sufficient resolution will get a man to heaven or hell."

"But you said he had a good sporting chance," I protested.

"Quite so. But a chance, however promising, isn't the same as a certainty, and he couldn't face the possible alternative." It had been a case, I recalled, of embezzlement on a big scale, with a very heavy penalty if he was found guilty. "I couldn't guarantee an acquittal, no defending counsel can do that. And certainly Bull, for the prosecution, lived up to his name. Any gate he butted would have been smithereens in a matter of minutes. My chap presumably felt he couldn't stand up to the cross-examination Bull certainly wouldn't have spared him." He sighed.

"I wish I'd known you were coming," I said remorsefully. "I'd have got you a steak or something."

"And now the choice is between poached eggs and beans on toast? Do women never flatter their palates? I'll ring through to Joe's and book a table in, say, half an hour."

I was becoming obsessed with a sickening fear that I wouldn't be able to get through the evening without self-betrayal. I could plead a headache, but Aubrey knew I never had headaches without good cause. I had a vision of myself in that accursed room, my arm rising and falling. I knew now what people mean when they talk of seeing red: one swims in a red mist and doesn't feel responsible for one's action. But I knew how much sympathy that sort of argument would get from Aubrey. "People who're not answerable for their actions should be in asylums," he'd say.

And yet, so adaptable is the human creature that when we were eating Joe's admirable entrecôte steaks and drinking his unpretentious but always sound wine, the evening began to feel like any other. Aubrey always brought back tidbits of information, what in my sex would have been called gossip; I had had letters, and exchanges with neighbors. The evening slipped past. We didn't speak of Peters again. One of the secrets of his profession, Aubrey had said, is to know when to shut the door and move on. What he couldn't explain to me was what you did if the door opened a crack and a ghost came slipping out, following you like a shadow down your prosperous roads, confronting you at a crossroad—because you can't slay a ghost.

When I went up to bed I found my eyes searching the treads of the stairs as if I might find the missing earring there; I even opened the white morocco jewelbox Aubrey had given me, in case, in some miraculous fantastic fashion, I had gone out wearing only one. But there was no sign of it anywhere, of course.

Aubrey was never one to sit about and wait for things to happen, cases to fall into his lap. Now that the Peters case had folded up on him, it wouldn't be long before he was engaged on something else. I heard him talking on the telephone as I made the breakfast coffee. Our Mrs. Day didn't come in till Aubrey had gone or was shut in his study. He didn't mention Peters or his disappointment; I knew he never would again.

As soon as he left the house I set out on my deplorable quest, trying to assure myself that I'd come home with my earring in my pocket. It was a fresh morning and early-morning hope waved in my heart like the first green tassels of spring on the trees in our square. As I walked down Piccadilly, I heard my name called, and there was Mary Connor, a cousin of Aubrey's. She was up from the country on a day ticket, wearing a handsome Saxony wool suit and handmade shoes. Mary's the sort who won't take no for an answer, and when she insisted that I should join her for coffee, I didn't put up much of a protest. Truth to tell, I didn't mind postponing my horrible interview for a bit longer. Besides, if I waited till after midday, I should be less noticeable. Mary's the best company in the world. I took no notice of the clock till she cried, "Look at the time. I had a date at twelve and it's past that now. It's your lively tongue, Meg. You've upset all my calculations."

Still laughing, she collected her belongings, insisted on paying for both coffees and ran for Fortnum and Mason. I made my way to Euston, amazed at the crowds on escalators and platforms—it was like being in the middle of a mart.

In Edgeways Street the doors of the Teapot and Dormouse were swinging busily. This was the lunch hour, the busy period. Most of the tables in the saloon bar were occupied by customers eating cheese rolls or pieces of pie. At the counter two men with derby hats on the backs of their heads discussed racing; just beyond them, perched on an inadequate stool, was a commercial type in a brown suit so bright in tone it set the teeth on edge. He looked as if he'd been poured into his clothes, as plump as a Toby jug. Common sense told me that the barman wouldn't recognize me, though I had been here twice previously within three days, but all the same I tried to look away. I needn't have bothered. If he noticed my existence, he paid me no attention, not even to the extent of taking my order. Certainly he was busy, and there was a certain amount of rather dismal verbal slapstick going on. After three or four minutes I felt so conspicuous I decided to slip away and make my inquiries by telephone, but as I half turned, the Brown Type turned also on his counter stool, saying in a voice as rich as the color of his suit, "Don't be like that, Sugar. Plenty of room. And Sam's bosses don't like him turning away custom. Ain't that true, Sam?"

I thought Sam would throw a glass of swipes in his face, and I could hardly have blamed him if he had, but to my amazement a sort of sulky grin spread itself over his face.

The B.T. patted an adjacent stool in a possessive sort of way. "Take a pew, Sugar."

My head was whirling. So this is a pickup, I thought. But I quickly ordered my brandy, following it up by adding, "I wanted to inquire about an earring I may have dropped here last night."

This seemed to startle even the Brown Type, who until now had seemed impervious to any change of atmosphere. The grin vanished immediately from Sam's face; he looked outraged as he turned to fulfill my order.

"Be your age, Sam," advised the fat man, who seemed to be a privileged person. "Lady has to ask. Insurance, see."

Sam put down the brandy, his sulkiness abating not one jot, and curtly told me the price—as if I didn't know. I had a momentary fear my companion might offer to settle for me, but apparently the notion hadn't gone through his head.

"Wherever the lady lost the earring, it wasn't here," said Sam.

"I have to ask," I pointed out crisply. "This is only one place among a number. Just as I have to report it to the police."

Sam's head came up with a jerk. "You can keep that flicking lot off my doorstep," he cried aggressively. "Well, Mr. Crook, you know what happens when it gets around that the fuzz are hanging about your premises."

"Surely you've nothing to hide, Sam," Mr. Crook teased him. (Why should the name sound vaguely familiar? I'd never seen him before, I was sure. He had round brown eyes like brandy balls and made me think of Mr. Magoo.)

"It's not me, Mr. Crook, nor you, but I can't be answerable for anyone who drops in and fancies a pint. Much as my license is worth to refuse him."

"Occupational hazard, Sam," said Mr. Crook cheerfully. "Same like it might amuse some villain to ram the Superb on my way home."

"Sooner ram a battleship than that jalopy," snorted Sam.

"Never insult a lady," warned the B.T.

Then the door of the saloon was pushed open and four or five men came tumbling noisily in.

"Place getting a mite crowded," offered Mr. Crook, picking up his glass. "Ever hear about the genius of the general? He always knew when to retreat."

There was a small table vacant against the wall, and he made for it, glass in hand, newspaper under his arm. It was a midday edition, I noticed, and doubtless he was a bookie's runner or one of those men who pass tips in public houses. But he was also my comfort and strength as of now, so I picked up my glass and followed him.

"The earring's very important to me," I heard myself explain. "My husband gave it to me, he had it specially designed."

"Hubby know it's lost?" asked Mr. Crook.

"I thought if I could find it, there was no need to bother him," I answered confusedly. "I thought there was just a chance that someone might have picked it up here and handed it over the counter, or even taken it to the police station."

"You have to be joking," said Mr. Crook. "Half the chaps who come in here—no, I tell a lie, four fifths of them—would sooner walk a mile in a blizzard than even go past the copper shop except on the other side of the street. Doing a bit of slumming, Sugar? I mean, this don't look like your home from home."

"I came to see an old servant of ours," I explained awkwardly. Etta would have exploded to hear me. "She's married and living in this part of London."

"Meet her here? Well, she's married a right cock, I'd say. What can't they pay for this time? The new jalopy, or the color TV?"

"They've got a great opportunity to go to the States," I blurted out. "She has relations there."

"The things we do to our old ally!" sighed Mr. Crook. "Suit your book nice, would it? What does hubby think? Yours, I mean, not hers."

"Oh, he doesn't know her," I said quickly, too quickly. "This was before we were married."

I saw his eyes on my plain slim wedding ring. "That wasn't put on yesterday," he said. "Lady putting the black on you, Sugar?"

I gasped at him. "Why on earth . . . what makes you think . . . ? What an extraordinary thing to say."

"No more extraordinary than finding you on your owney-oh in the Dormouse. As for why, well, she's asking the favors, ain't she? So Mahomet should go to the mountain." I gave a shudder at the notion of Etta coming near our house on Campden Hill. "When the mountain comes visiting Mahomet, that's the time to look out for squalls. Now tell me I'm nosy," he went on, with no change of voice. "I wouldn't disagree. But

99

I was born that way." He certainly carried a pretty striking specimen about with him. He shook out his newspaper. "No offense, Sugar."

He didn't sound remotely offended on his part. I was shocked at myself. He hadn't been trying to pick me up, he just wanted to be kind. And then I knew where I'd heard his name before. Mr. Dowler—*a man, still I understand on the Law List, called Crook, whose clients are always innocent.* And I'd thought, I'd never get him on legal aid, he'd have them standing in queues a mile deep. He must have been observing me, for all his apparent absorption in his paper, for he said now, "Finish that, Sugar and have the other half. If some single drinks were kitties the R.S.P.C.A. 'ud step in to stop 'em being put on the market so young. Follow the gee-gees? No? There's one called Feet of Brass fancied for the three-thirty, but not by me."

He went toward the counter, where the crowd was two deep. I picked up his newspaper, not much liking to be a woman sitting alone in such a place even for a minute. I glanced at the paragraphs not concerned with the gee-gees.

I didn't hear Mr. Crook come back. I'd forgotten his existence. I'd forgotten everyone except Aubrey and Gavin, and everything except what I was going to do to them now. Vaguely I heard the clatter of a glass set down.

"So you can do it without the crystal ball," said Mr. Crook's voice, genial as a summer breeze. And at that I lifted my head. He picked up the glass and pushed it quickly into my hand. "You can't go fainting in a place like this," he said. "It ain't fair to Sam. I thought you said you didn't play the gee-gees."

"I don't," I confirmed, letting the paper fall. "I just saw something about someone I used to know. It's a bit of a shock." I could hear my words falling out like water from a cracked bucket. The last thing I wanted to do was talk to this (or any) stranger about Etta, Etta who'd been found last night in Klondyke Street, with her head battered, her bag open and a flick knife on the table beside her. Mr. Crook took the paper from my nerveless hand. His bright brown eyes flickered over it like a swift-moving beetle.

"This couldn't be the ex-slavey you went to see?" he murmured softly. "No, don't tell me. I always say Providence has a pattern, and you tell me what I'm doing in this sleazy joint if there ain't some good reason behind it." He read a little more. "Lady took in typing. That's original anyway. Mostly it's modeling or even massage, but you do generally have to show a diploma for that. Seems to have been the adventurous type," he went on calmly. "That's for you to drink, Sugar, not drop tears into. Flick knife, eh?"

"I'd never seen one before," I burst out.

"If I'd had as many hot dinners as I've seen flick knives . . . Hey, Sugar, what's that you said? What were you doing in—where was it?—Klondyke Street last night? Rough kind of night from the sound of it. Tape recorder bashed, phone put out of commish—seems like someone was trying to ransack the apartment."

"She was all right when I left her," I insisted. "I know about the recorder and she showed me the flick knife, but when I left, she was all right."

"Any special reason for being there at all?" Mr. Crook asked. "Oh yes, she was putting the black on you. Best thing to do in those circumstances is bring up your big battalions."

"I haven't got any big battalions," I protested.

"I bet Aubrey Fielding wouldn't be flattered to hear you say that. Now, take it easy, Sugar. Of course I knew who you were. I read the papers, don't I? And you haven't changed much. If you want a sympathetic jury in a murder trial," he added, "you want to be as ugly as sin. That gives the jurors a sense of superiority, see, and that's what they enjoy. Remember the brass candlestick?"

"I smashed the tape recorder with it, but I never laid a finger on her. And she was expecting someone else when I left. Oh!"

"Remembered something, Sugar?"

"They'll have my fingerprints on the candlestick. I wasn't wearing gloves."

"So?"

"They'll have my fingerprints from that other time."

"No, why?" asked Mr. Crook. "You got a Not Guilty verdict, didn't you? So the prints 'ull have been destroyed. Mind you, some countries 'ud keep 'em on record forever, but not us. We do like to give the underdog a chance."

"She asked for it," I said bluntly. "Sooner or later it was bound to happen. If not here, then in New York."

"In her line of business, sudden death's an occupational risk." Nothing seemed to shake this extraordinary man.

"I don't know who you are," I heard myself say.

"Till you've been cautioned, it don't matter what you tell me," Mr. Crook pointed out. "No witnesses, see?"

An appalling thought struck me. "You—you're not connected with the police?"

He put back his head and roared. The flimsy walls of the Dormouse seemed to shake. "Ask them and see their faces turn red."

He pulled something out of his pocket; it looked like one of those large advertisements of car-hire firms that you find pushed into your letterbox. I picked it up. It was more like a much magnified visiting card. It said: *Arthur G. Crook*—with two addresses, one in Bloomsbury and one in Earls Court. I said, "I used to live in Earls Court before I married—my first marriage, I mean. I expect it's changed a lot now."

Mr. Crook looked surprised. "Changed? A mite more people maybe, a mite more color all round the clock. But it was always a dormitory town. I couldn't ask for better."

I went back to scanning the card. *Your Trouble Our Busi-*

ness, it said. And *We Never Close.* And *Answering Service Day and Night.*

"Is it a joke?" I asked.

"Not to me and Bill it ain't. It's our daily bread. Now, not touting for custom of course, Sugar, have me off the list like winking if even a whisper went round, but no harm you putting that card in your purse and maybe sometime you might find a use for it. Give you a piece of advice, free, gratis and for nothing," he went on. "Don't answer any questions, whoever puts them, without you have your lawyer present."

"I don't have a lawyer," I said.

"Married to one of the best. Pardon me if I'm speaking out of turn."

"I couldn't tell him," I cried, shocked. "Anyway, why should anyone link me up with this?"

"Not confided in the girl friend?"

"I couldn't speak of this to anyone. Her husband knew I was there, because she told me he always had a list of her visitors, just to be on the safe side. But he's not likely to come forward. It would tie him up with her racket. She called herself by her maiden name in Klondyke Street, but his name is Porter."

"He was the one who found her," Mr. Crook told me. "Bothered when she didn't come back around eight, like she said; couldn't get any answer, so went round and there she was. Bit of a shock even to the most casual ever-loving."

"How do they start that sort of business?" I wondered. "Blackmailing, I mean. She was a secretary at a hotel in the West Country—the Royal Marmaduke. No," I corrected myself, "she was a chambermaid there, but she moved on to another hotel as secretary to residents and visitors. It was very interesting."

"I'll say," agreed Mr. Crook. "Not many better ways of getting info about a chap's private life, specially if you're sharp at mental arithmetic, as I daresay she was. Two and two and two and two make a hundred and four added up the right way. I knew a parlormaid once," he went on. "That dates me, don't it? Magpies weren't in it with her. A bit here and a bit there. So trustworthy, so don't bother to lock up your mail, and she'd never stoop to listen on the extension. Ho no! They say there's one born every minute, and they're fair game for the marauders. If that girl hadn't been careless . . . but that's what brings 'em all down in the end. I'm so tooting clever I'll never be found out. Afraid you may have dropped your earring on her premises? Well, you didn't come all this way for a drop of fourth-rate O.D.V. Got you on toast, hasn't she? I feel sorry for nicely brought up dames, they don't get a chance. It's wrastle, gouge and rabbit-punch all the way in this wicked world, this part of it anyhow, and though I daresay they taught you to dance nice and play the piano, no one told you how to twist a lady's arm or give a chap one or two rousers below the belt. You take my word for it, Sugar, Mrs. Etta Porter knew her way around blindfolded. So well, she thought she could invent a new rule or two on her own. What she didn't twig was that they've all been tried, and if they ain't been adopted by the sorority, it's because they don't pay off."

"What do we do now?" I asked.

"If you're asking my advice, which you ain't, seeing I ain't your man of affairs, I'd say tell your husband. Well, what are husbands for?"

"I couldn't do that," I said at once. "For the moment, anyhow, I shall let sleeping dogs lie."

"Trouble with sleeping dogs is they will talk in their sleep. You must have heard them, whimpering and pushing, dropping a hint here and a growl there."

"You don't understand," I protested.

"Not being the Lord God," acknowledged Mr. Crook piously, "I wouldn't presume to understand the way any dame's mind worked."

"So what do I do now?" I demanded.

"Same like I said. Wait. Patience is a law of nature. Think of all those birds sitting on their eggs for days and days waiting to hear 'em pop. Murder's a waiting game, too."

"But how do we find out the truth?" I couldn't leave it at that.

"We don't, Sugar. It ain't our job. That's what we pay the police for, and they ain't going to thank you, poking your proboscis in where it ain't wanted. Let them find out the name of the one who was expected after you. Let them discover who'd been threatening the lady to such an extent that she was prepared to uproot herself and take off for the States."

"You think she was being blackmailed, too?" It was a new idea to me.

"Well, I don't know, do I?" said Mr. Crook reasonably. "But the way of the transgressor is hard—remember? Think of all the anonymous callers on the buzzer telling you how they're going to rip out your tripes, all the veiled dames waiting round corners with tubes of vitriol. Lady, when St. Paul said his piece about standing in jeopardy every hour, he didn't know the half. Well, Sugar"—he began to rise, a round barrel of a man, the sort that make such good dancers—"I see my contact's come in." (He was sitting with his back to the door, but there was a scrap of looking glass on the opposite wall.) "Can't keep him waiting. Well, I hope you didn't think I came here for the beer. They're the shyest chaps in the business, flutter back to the bushes at a breath if you can't catch their coat sleeve first, and you could ladder every nylon you possessed before you found out the bush where they were hiding. And that's something to keep in mind. They carry a load of trouble same like you. People ain't sorry enough for sinners; say what you like, the dice are loaded against them, and it never seemed much comfort to me that it's their own fault."

He had collected his man and had him up at the bar before I had put on my gloves.

I half expected to find an anonymous letter in the box on my return, but there was only the usual trade trash. And though the telephone rang several times, the caller always gave his or her identity without hesitation. Most of them were for Aubrey, anyway. I tried to comfort myself with the thought that if the police had found an earring in Etta's room, they either had no way of tracing the owner or were waiting for her to come forward. So far as I was concerned, they could wait till the day of doom. All the same, when I went to stand at the window for a minute to watch the vegetable cart go by about five-thirty and caught sight of a policeman in uniform, I began to shake like someone with palsy. It didn't occur to me until later that if I was going to be charged or even seriously questioned, they'd send a crime squad car, not just an ordinary bobby on the beat.

The evening paper came a few minutes afterward. There seemed to be trouble all over the world, but only the local trouble interested me. There wasn't much fresh about Etta— Gerald didn't know about her clients, sometimes she worked late on a special job, they'd been planning to go abroad and she was clearing things up. He had gone around when she didn't arrive by eight-thirty, and after calling the police, had sat on the stairs in the hall with one of the other tenants, a man called Fitzgerald, until the authorities arrived. The police believed the candlestick could have been the weapon used, which argued a crime of impulse, since a deliberate murderer would take his weapon with him. The police were anxious to interview a woman who had been seen on the steps of No. 14 about seven o'clock that night.

I put the paper down very, very gently. So someone had noticed me, after all. The two Pakistanis? But they were talking like rival streams. The girl in love? But she hadn't even looked in my direction. Someone from one of the houses opposite, most likely. Windows in houses like those are always discreetly curtained, and behind them, like beaming human blowflies, sit the curious, the rejected, the non-participants. I told myself to keep my head. No one could have seen me well enough to recognize me again or even recall what I wore. I was in the clear, I thought, so long as I kept my mouth shut.

If by some mischance I was approached, I could say I had seen Gerald haunting the mouth of the alley. He hadn't mentioned that to the police. Only here doubts set in. I'd said, That's Gerald, but could I be absolutely sure? My first thought had been that he was so like a score of others, you might mistake him in broad daylight. I hadn't been able to see the watch chain. Perhaps it wasn't Gerald, after all. The man I'd seen leaving the house hadn't come forward with the information that a woman, carrying a file, had come about six-thirty, asking for Mrs. Cusack. I hadn't come forward with my evidence. Gerald, too, seemed to be lying pretty low. The fact was, we were all like the muzzled ox grinding the alien corn, all tethered by fear. I even began to feel sorry for the police.

During the two days that followed my encounter with Mr. Crook, I felt myself stiffen every time the doorbell rang and I heard Mrs. Day go along the hall. When the telephone shrilled I was quick to lift the receiver, in case she thought I hadn't heard and answered for me. She was very good at taking telephone messages, and whenever I came in I would look hurriedly and apprehensively at the pad in the hall, but the only recorded messages seemed straightforward enough.

On the third day I told myself I was getting into a frightful stew for nothing. If I couldn't move against Gerald, he couldn't move against me. I'd been acting on the assumption that he would have found my earring and was perhaps keeping it to carry on the good work where Etta had laid it down, but what proof had I that I hadn't dropped it somewhere in the street? Or even that someone hadn't picked it up in the Dormouse and wasn't talking? In any case, I couldn't be the only woman who visited Etta at her business address.

Then, when I had talked myself into a mood of reason, it

happened. The bell rang, I picked up the telephone confidently, expecting the caller to be Phyllis Paston, who sat on the same hospital committee as I did, but the voice that answered me wasn't a woman's.

"Mrs. Fielding? I wonder if you've lost anything of value lately?"

"Who's speaking?" I asked. As if I didn't know.

"Such as an earring," insinuated the voice. You could say that for the Porters, they pulled no punches.

"Are you trying to find an owner?" I asked.

"I thought it might be quicker—and more convenient—to approach you direct. Of course, I could take it along to the Euston police, if you prefer."

"Wouldn't they wonder at you having waited so long? It would save everyone trouble if you put it in an envelope and posted it."

"It's rather a valuable object to put in the post," Gerald demurred. "Must mean a lot to you, seeing your husband designed it. How would it be if I was to bring it round? Then we could settle matters on the spot."

"No reward's being offered," I said. A braver woman, I suppose, would have called his bluff, told him to take his find to the police and explain how he'd known it was mine. But he wouldn't do that, any more than I would tell Aubrey the truth.

"Think about it," Gerald offered. "I'll call again about three."

"I don't expect to be in," I assured him.

"Then I'll have to chance it, won't I?"

I heard a small greasy chuckle, and then the connection was cut.

8

I went up to my room and found the card Mr. Crook had given me, then I rang his number. A strange mechanical voice answered: "This is Bloomsbury 10,000. The proprietor is not in, but if you will leave a message it will be relayed to him on his return. Please speak slowly, give your name, address and telephone number. Thank you."

I had never spoken on an answering phone before. I stopped twice in the middle of what I was saying to ask "Have you got that?" and "Is that all right?" It seemed strange when no one replied. I left my message. "I shall be coming in about three o'clock," I said defiantly.

Mr. Crook had an office in Bloomsbury Street at the very top of a tall house with a view over a part of London I scarcely knew. It had a Dickensian atmosphere. Mr. Pecksniff or Mr. Micawber might have emerged from any of those narrow doorways, though for the most part these were now hotels and apartment houses. Students from various countries swarmed in and out and hurried up the street, making the staid old road look as colorful as an oriental bazaar. There were so many stairs I got tired of counting them—nothing so modern as a lift had been installed—and the last flight wasn't even carpeted. Mr. Crook explained later in his casual and engaging way that if clients realized they had to climb so far, they'd think twice about wasting his time, and the advantage of a naked stair was that you could hear feet on it and be prepared for any emergency. His must have been the least orderly and comfortable office in London. Papers and files occupied the tables and chairs, though I never saw him refer to one, even when our conversation was interrupted by some telephone call urgent enough for his partner Bill Parsons to put it through. He sat there like a huge brown-bottle, if you can imagine such a fly, and displayed not a scrap of surprise at my appearance.

"Bella gave me your message," he said, nodding toward the ansaphone. I supposed she'd been called after the famous Bell who invented the telephone. "Reckoned you'd find your way here sooner or later. Didn't fall over a bucket or anything?"

That was a reference to the workmen who were doing structual repairs on the entrance floor. It was one of them who, seeing me hesitate, had said instantly, "Looking for Mr. Crook, love? Right on and up the stairs." And they all laughed, but not in a surprised way. I supposed they were used to seeing strangers walk in because they were in trouble.

I said no, I hadn't fallen over anything yet, but things were hotting up, and I told him about Gerald's message.

"You told me not to speak to anyone till I'd consulted my lawyer," I said.

"And you reckon that's what you're doing now?"

"I reckon," I told him.

"Taken your time, haven't you?" he said, offering me the hardest chair in London as though it were a throne. "Still, not to worry. Given us a chance to do a bit of our homework."

"You mean, you knew I'd come?"

Mr. Crook spread his enormous hands. "Where else, Sugar, seeing you were all set against letting hubby into the act? Came through this morning, did he?"

"And is probably trying to get through again at this minute."

"Mention his name?"

"No. But I recognized his voice. He was ringing from a call box," I added.

"Shows his sense. Difficult to trace that kind."

"What I don't understand is what he expects to get out of it. I warned Etta I couldn't raise another pound."

"Maybe he has ideas about your husband."

"Aubrey wouldn't give him a brass farthing," I declared. "He'd be far more likely to go straight to the police."

Mr. Crook looked dubious. "Well, but would he, Sugar? If you made him a present of all the facts? Wife being black-mailed seizes brass candlestick and whacks out at tape recorder. Next step is whacking out at the lady herself."

A new thought struck me. "If I'd attacked her, wouldn't I have got blood all over me?"

"Candlestick have a sharp point? I thought as much. Couple of sharp dents 'ud do it. Most of the bleeding was internal anyway. How about you starting at the beginning, Sugar? You didn't say how you came to meet up with your ex-slavey again."

I explained about the postcard, the first meeting at the Teapot and Dormouse, resulting in my call in Klondyke Street.

"And you never said nuffin' to no one?"

I shook my head.

"Who's got this famous letter now?"

"No one. It's destroyed."

He didn't look as pleased as I'd hoped. "Postcard ditto?"

"You couldn't expect me to keep that," I exploded.

"Nothing to tie you in with the murder at all, then?"

"Only Gerald, and I don't see how he can come forward. He can't even be sure it's my earring. I was wearing a scarf at the Dormouse that night, and I didn't take it off. Of course, there's that barman. He might remember a strange woman asking about an earring."

"Chaps like Sam are too fly to go looking for trouble. No, if Porter was so sure it was yours, and if he wasn't he wouldn't have rung, there's only one answer, and your guess is as good as mine. Come on, Sugar, make with the loaf."

"You mean," I discovered, "he knew because Etta had told him."

"Told him with bells on, I should think."

"He said something about knowing it was made to order. He couldn't have known that . . . So it *was* him I saw at the mouth of the alley."

"Waiting for the entrance of the third fly, no doubt," agreed Crook. "Sure it was him, Sugar? That's the sort of thing the police are apt to be fussy about. And all cats in the dark look gray. You can bet he'll have an alibi all wool and a yard wide. Lady must have been a bit daft," he added. "It's like I said, they get too sure of themselves. Never expected violence from you."

"I was surprised at myself," I acknowledged, "and she kept screaming put that down, put that down. I must admit," I added in a sudden burst of confidence, "if she'd suddenly dropped dead at my feet, I'd probably have danced a cachuka for joy."

"Same being sort of a pagan ritual? Not a dancin' man myself. No, whoever did this had come prepared to do it, whether he or she—it could easy be a woman—knows it or not. Murder starts in the mind. When some God-fearing citizen says to himself 'When Aunt Bessie dies I'll strike it rich' instead of 'If the old girl kicks the bucket in the next five years' . . . that's the time to look out for squalls. I don't go much for these impulsive murders myself. If a chap takes a weapon with him, he can say till he's blue in the face that he's only carrying it for defensive purposes, but I wouldn't believe him and nor would the fuzz. No man goes out armed unless he's prepared to make use of whatever it is. Now, it ain't likely two clients would go berserk with the same weapon on the same night, though that don't mean it couldn't happen. But if I was the fuzz, I'd be searching in drains and on rubbish tips and among car cemeteries for something that might just have put paid to madame's account. And for all I know, that's just what the fuzz is doing. But there's a lot of drains and car cemeteries and it all takes time. Now, like I said, we've been doing our homework. Bill put a fellow on to inquire into the lady's past, always useful to have a few cards up your sleeve. You put us on the trail, telling us about the Royal Marmaduke, and Bill's come up with some very interesting facts, very interesting indeed."

He picked up a sheet of paper, at random it seemed to me, but clearly it was the one he wanted. "From the Marmaduke she moved to the Royal Edward."

"Do you always go to so much trouble, even when you know you may not be called in?" I asked curiously.

"You get kind of a hunch," Crook told me. "Well, Madam Etta worked at this Royal Edward hotel for nearly three years, then she married a local, bit of a big wig from what one can make out. More likely a good-sized frog in a small pond. But I'll tell you this, the match wasn't expected and it wasn't much liked. Tracy—that was the chap's name— no, I don't know yet where Porter comes in, unless he changed it by Deed Poll—was believed to have his eye on a local young lady, but it was Etta Cusack who said I will. She'd been acting as this Tracy's secretary," he added casually. "Like I said, there's no better way of digging a bit of dirt about your employer. There was an account of the nuptials in the local rag, picture of the happy couple. Bill got a blow-up reproduction." He opened a drawer and pulled out a good-sized envelope. "Take a peek, Sugar. Hey, what gives?"

For I was staring at the photograph as if my eyes would fall out. "You're quite right," I agreed. "This isn't Gerald Porter. This is the man who nearly fell over me on the top step at 14 Klondyke Street a few days ago."

"They say surprise is the spice of life," recalled Mr. Crook after a breathless moment. "You're sartin sure, Sugar?"

"I was never surer of anything."

"Then I'll tell you something else. There's a record of this wedding to Tracy, quite apart from the press, but Bill can't track down a hint of divorce."

"Perhaps there never was one. That would mean she and Porter aren't really married."

"And perhaps," Crook said, "Tracy married again thinking she'd gone through with a divorce. Perhaps that's what she had on him."

"Well, anyway, he's not the one who killed her, because she was alive when I went in. Why," I discovered, "I'm his only alibi. I'm the only one who can show he's bound to be innocent."

"Riding a bit in front of the hounds, ain't you?" drawled Mr. Crook. "He could have come back."

But I didn't believe that.

"Do the police know this?" I wondered.

"The police and me ain't on what you might call intimate terms, but it wouldn't surprise me. You have to be up pretty early in the morning to put one over on the fuzz."

"Then how do you do it?" I asked. I really wanted to know.

Mr. Crook opened his big eyes till they looked like tea plates. "Simple, Sugar. Just don't go to bed."

"If they do trace him, he's bound to tell them he saw me."

"Didn't give him your moniker, I suppose?"

It took a second for the meaning to sink in. Then I said, "No. No, of course I didn't."

"And you weren't draped in mink or walking on stilts or carrying a teddy bear, nothing to catch his attention like. And the same goes for the lady who told the police she'd seen a young woman on the step about seven o'clock. We mayn't be the freest country in the world any more, but it's no crime to stand on a doorstep." He lifted his voice. "Bill!" He called.

The door opened and a man came in, tall, with a face that

was handsome before a long scar ruined it. But he was in his own way as formidable as Crook.

"Meet our client in the Porter case," invited Mr. Crook amiably.

I might have been a fly that had settled on the arm of the chair for all the notice Bill took of me. "You got all the gen, didn't you, Bill? Any mention of an evening edition, late evening edition, that 'ud be, found in the room in Klondyke Street?"

"If it was, the fuzz are keeping it to themselves," said Bill.

"Of course," continued Mr. Crook, "if you'd just battered your common-law wife with a poker, you might just forget about the paper. Still, even if there was one there, anyone could have brought it. Evening editions are on the street from about three o'clock."

Bill drifted away, impersonal as a breeze. I knew a sudden gust of impatience. "So now," I said, "what? No, don't tell me. We wait. But who for? What for?"

"For X to make the next move," said Mr. Crook. "Well, someone's got to make it, and how can it be us when we don't know what direction we're going in? Know how it is the police net so many villains? Because they're a body of patient men. Presently they'll turn up a snout or the invisible witness will put in an appearance . . ."

"The invisible witness?"

"Don't know where any of us 'ud be without him. He's the chap you can't allow for when you're laying your plans, because you don't know he exists. I remember when I was a younger man than I am now, a husband who couldn't stand the eternal nag-nag of the wife of his buzoom, so he pushed her through a window. Cul-de-sac, two A.M., no one around, you'd think that was safe. Lady a moon worshiper, must have bowed too low. Only it happened that another chap wearing the same pair of shoes decided to go for a walk to stop himself cleaving his old lady's head open with a meat axe. And just as he passed the end of the cul-de-sac, kersplosh, down she floated. Maybe someone else saw Porter buying a paper or opening a front door or leaving a house at a convenient hour, and ain't got round to telling the police yet. Sooner or later X'll start to feel safe and that's when chaps put their necks into the noose, figuratively speaking. Or they get cold feet and run to the copper shop to have them warmed up.

"Read criminal history, you'd be surprised how many chaps can't stand the strain, specially the amateurs, have to talk to someone, general public's out because they can't be trusted, so what's left except the fuzz? Or he may lose his nerve, tries to make his posish safer, works up a false alibi if awkward questions should be asked, and that's the most fatal of all, because what man hath built, the C.I.D. can unbuild. So—we don't try to get in touch with Gerald Porter, we let him make the first move. He's come out of his hole by admitting he's got the earring; he can't leave the country till the mystery's been either cleared or shelved—maybe the fuzz has something else against him he's forgotten to mention. Now, if he comes through on the blower, you act like you were the *au pair* girl. Wrong number, *chéri*. So you go home, Sugar, don't accept lifts from strange men and keep a chain on your door. Now I've got to go and see a chap who wants me to prove he was in Gateshead when half the police force know he was in Battersea on the site of a certain warehouse."

The atmosphere in Mr. Crook's office had become so involved and the possibilities his words had aroused seemed so murky, I was surprised to find it was a bright day in the streets, a thin but resolute sunlight painting the pavements and illuminating the green buds of the plane trees that grew along the edge of the pavement. An elderly man in a Harold Macmillan fur hat, carrying a white Pekinese puppy, made me stop. The puppy wore a gold bow and might have been going to a fairy wedding. I was just going to compliment the man on his companion when I remembered Mr. Crook's advice to trust no one—though I couldn't believe Gerald had set this up just for my benefit. Life was going to be pretty grim if I had to suspect the most casual passer-by.

In the front garden of our house there is a wooden seat. I never quite understood why it should be there, since the view is only that of a London street, but one day when I went out I found an old man sitting there. He looked up as I closed the door, very polite, almost eager, but not in the least embarrassed at being found on private property. In spite of all the warnings the police issue so assiduously to ignorant and credulous householders, I couldn't believe he was part of a gang out to "case the joint."

"It's a nice seat you've put here, lady," he said. "It's not everyone would think of putting a seat where an old chap can rest his bones. Do you know"—he spoke like someone who wanted to give me information—"there's no seat along this road for nigh a mile, bar this. It's peaceful to sit here and watch the world go by."

No, I couldn't be suspicious of him, even though I know this is the age of the little man, and who's likely to suspect an old boy in a raincoat and a tweed hat, resting for a few minutes, most likely till the pubs opened? Soon he was as familiar to me as the robin that used to hop on what the house agent called the patio on the other side of the house. If he hadn't turned up at least once a week, I should have been quite concerned. He never asked for food or even for a glass of water. He didn't stay long either, he was one of those rare people for whom it isn't necessary to feel a grain of pity. In fact, he lightened rather than increased the normal load.

So when I rounded the corner of the street I was always prepared to see him and always pleased when I did. I knew he found our seat a convenient place to wait till the opening of the Fig and Thistle in Makepeace Street, which was a kind of club to him. Even my rather prim Mrs. Day could find nothing against him. "He's not forever bothering to help bring in the fuel or shift the dustbin," she confided. "They're the ones to watch out for. Nobody does anything for nothing, so what are they looking for? Mr. James is just a decent body, and if he likes to sit there and you've no objection, well, I'm sure I haven't." I don't think Aubrey ever saw him. He had always faded away before then.

This afternoon, when I came back from Mr. Crook's office, the seat was occupied, but not by Mr. James. As I opened the gate Gerald Porter stood up and grinned. The sun shone on the little gold fish swinging on his watch chain.

"I rang at three," he said sunnily. "No reply."

There wouldn't be, of course. This was Mrs. Day's afternoon off.

"I did warn you," I said.

"So I thought I'd come along in person—just to see if you could identify it."

A neighbor passed and looked curiously over the gate. Ours is a friendly neighborhood, we all have a word for one another, though we don't all exchange names. We recognize people by their dogs, cats and cars. It's quite usual for Aubrey to say, "Old Riley went past this morning." Or, "There's a new young MG sporting type at No. 42." Once when we had a cat for a short time, I even got an invitation to drinks addressed to Mrs. Sam. I knew this particular woman, she was a great chatterbox, known locally as the Daily Post. I said reluctantly to Gerald, "It's getting a bit chilly. You'd better come in."

I wasn't expecting Aubrey back for some time, I hoped no one else would have a notion of calling. I took Gerald into the small room at the back that I call my sewing room. I wasn't going to have him in any of the rooms that belonged to Aubrey and myself. The sewing room, in a sense, was neutral ground.

Gerald looked about him in leisurely fashion. "Nice place

you have here," he offered. He didn't look in the least like a new-made widower (well, I suppose, in a sense he wasn't), a man whose official wife had been brutally murdered a few days before. I thought, irrationally, Only a guilty man could preserve such a confident air. He put his hand into his pocket and drew out a little wash-leather bag.

"Is this it?" he asked, shaking my earring into the palm of his hand.

"It might be," I agreed cautiously. "It's remarkably like it."

"Don't give me that," he said. "You told Etta it was unique, made to your husband's order."

"Is that what she told you?"

"Isn't it true, then?"

"What I mean is, it proves she was all right when I left the apartment, because I'd only just told her. So you either saw or spoke to her after I did. Mr. Crook will be very interested to know that."

Gerald whistled. "You must be in a bit of a stew to have pulled him in," he offered.

"It's not very well looked on to have your own next-of-kin to represent you, even in emergencies," I said.

"What advice did _he_ give you?"

"He told me to discuss nothing to do with Etta's death without my lawyer being present."

It gave me the famous ring of confidence to say those words—my lawyer. Years ago, in a little country church, I walked up into the pulpit, and at once I understood how it is that young men, new to the ministry, can so confidently advise their elders, who had been fighting the good fight for half a century. I thought Gerald's face looked more thoughtful, and decided that the mention of Mr. Crook, with a capital "C" to this small-time operator, might make him watch his step. Or was he so conceited that he believed he could baffle even Mr. Crook?

"Playing safe?" Gerald asked.

"That's more than you're doing," I told him. "I think it shows a considerable if misguided courage to tangle with him at all. But then, your sort of life probably calls for that sort of spirit."

I saw I'd pinked him there. "You want to watch your tongue," he said. "It could get you into worse trouble still. You were there that night . . ."

"And she was all right when I'd gone, because she told you about the earring."

"Did I say that?" He sounded genuinely surprised.

"You know you did. How else did you know it was mine?"

"You'd just left her . . ."

"She had another visitor coming."

"You might find it hard to wish an earring on to that character."

"And so how did you know my husband had designed them?"

He lifted his mousy brows. "Did I? I thought you told me that."

I could see he was going to be about as safe to tangle with as a werewolf. "Do you always meet your wife's clients?" I asked.

"I know their names. I've got a Mr. Richard Smith coming to see me at six-thirty tonight." He put on a commendable imitation of Etta's voice. "How much does that tell me? There can't be more than a couple of hundred thousand of them knocking around. You were different. You see, Etta had once worked for you—you'd given the orders."

"That was hardly noticeable," I said.

"She didn't like to be remembered that way. She thought you might try to pull rank on that account. Very sensitive about rank, Etta was. But if she turned up, a married woman . . . plus husband."

"Well, not exactly," I murmured, and for the first time his face darkened.

"I warned you about that tongue of yours," he said. He half turned. "We must finish this conversation another time. By the way, that old chap who hangs around here."

"Old . . . ? Do you mean Mr. James?"

"I don't know what he calls himself. Looks as if he came out of a musical comedy chorus. I suppose you know something about him."

"Is that any concern of yours?" I demanded. "He happens to be an old man who likes to rest occasionally." Light broke suddenly. "Was he here today when you came? Do you mean to say you—you displaced him?" I found my voice was shaking with anger.

"Well, you didn't want an audience, did you? Old fellow pouring out a lot of hot air at the pub—Aubrey Fielding's wife, Lady Fielding before long, if rumor's correct. Still, not to worry, I doubt if he'll come back. Ever mention him to your husband?"

I hesitated, because I honestly couldn't remember.

Gerald sent me a knowing smile. "Mum's the word," he said, putting his stubby finger to his lips. "Now, I'll give you a day or two to think something up. Don't try and telephone or write. I'll be round."

"If Mr. Crook isn't round to see you first," I cried.

He shook his head confidently. "Whatever you are," he said, "you're not stupid. I said that to Etta the first night."

"I'm sorry I can't return the compliment," I told him. I really did think he was crazy, pitting himself against Mr. Crook. Then the telephone started to ring.

"You take it," said Gerald easily. "I can see myself out. Okay, I shan't lift anything en route. There's nothing much here except that copper bowl, and you'd need a mechanical grab to deal with that."

I watched him stroll through the hall and out the front

door. The telephone was still ringing. I snatched off the receiver.

"So you are still in the land of the living?" said a voice. "We've been waiting for you."

Too late I remembered an appointment I'd had with some of the locals—we were organizing a library service for a new nursing home for the aged that didn't come under National Health, anyway, not so far as amenities were concerned.

"I had an unexpected call," I explained. "I'll come along right away."

I scribbled a message for Aubrey in case he got back early, and went out. The meeting closed, as such meetings normally do, with sherry and general chat. So that when I returned, Aubrey was there already. He said calmly, "Someone's sending you billets-doux, by hand"—and he indicated an envelope on the table. It was an ordinary enough envelope, plain white commercial. I opened it—and my earring fell into my palm.

"It's come back," I exclaimed, conscious of Aubrey's eyes on me. "I lost it a day or two ago," I explained. "I didn't want to bother you because it might turn up again. And someone's found it and recognized it."

" 'Let not thy left hand know what thy right hand doeth,' " quoted Aubrey.

"They're pretty well recognized locally," I pointed out. "Half the shop assistants have asked me where I got them."

"Nice to know we've still got some honest people among us," Aubrey said, and for some reason that made me turn crimson. I didn't understand why Gerald had parted with his evidence, but I didn't think it was for any charitable motive. I decided to get in touch with Mr. Crook next day and take his advice.

Only, as it happened, I didn't.

9

I was supervising the breakfast coffee next morning when I heard an unusual sound from the dining room. My husband's voice cried, "So it's come at last. The silly fellow! Everyone warned him and he wouldn't listen to any of us. I suppose he thought he'd solved the problem of immortality. All the same," he added more temperately as I brought the tray into the room, "this is going to plunge a considerable section of the shadier part of society into mourning."

"Are you practicing your speech?" I murmured, pouring out his first cup. Then I saw his face, and my own changed. I'd no more inclination to flippancy. He wore a look of real grief. "What is it?" I cried.

He took the cup I handed him and set it down untouched. "A chap called Crook," he said, not lifting his eyes from the paper, as if he could compel it to reveal a bit more than was printed there. "Found concussed in the hall of his place of business in Bloomsbury Street last night by the constable on duty."

"I'll get the kidneys and bacon," I offered, needing a moment's respite.

"I'll tell you one thing," said Aubrey when I returned, too absorbed even to drink his coffee hot, "I wouldn't care to be the chap responsible. The police force has got its hands full as it is, they aren't going to have all the extra personnel they're going to need when the chap's identity becomes known. If he's got any sense, he'll be out of the country already."

"You mean, you think he was attacked?" I was pouring

my own coffee and my hand shook and a brown stream ran on to the cloth. Hurriedly I covered it with a plate.

"I don't think a knowing old bird like Crook just fell down a flight of stairs he's been mounting and dismounting for about thirty years, not through sheer carelessness. It says here"—he had absently taken a mouthful of kidneys and bacon and forgotten them again—"the bulb of the ground-floor light was found loosened. Bulbs don't loosen themselves. Ground floor out of commission for the moment on account of workmen, so it's not likely there'd be anyone on the spot to see what happened."

I didn't need to ask—I was pretty sure I knew. I could hear myself taunting Gerald about Mr. Crook. But he'd been right, I should watch my dangerous tongue.

"Might have been the workmen, of course," brooded Aubrey, the fair-minded. Only I knew it wasn't. "These chaps aren't always too careful how they muck around with things."

"You said concussed," I whispered. "Does that mean . . . ?"

"It means concussed. One thing, they want a constable on duty outside St. Edmunds, that's where they've taken him, trust the press to get on to that, if the news stays bad. I suppose Crook has a more efficient bodyguard than anyone bar the royal family."

"It doesn't seem to have saved him from getting concussed," I burst out.

"He's shown a remarkable capacity for looking after his own affairs to date. And of course, he's got that man, Bill Parsons, who wouldn't scruple to scalp the aggressor, and quite possibly anyone who tried to stop him."

"Is he a friend of yours?" I asked, a bit bewildered, because over the years I'd learned to distinguish between the various cadences of my husband's voice, and this wasn't just a normal anxiety—good chap pipped, that kind of thing—there was a personal ring in it that made me uncomfortable.

Aubrey looked surprised. "Didn't I ever say? It was through him I got into the Harding case ten years ago. I was feeling a bit huffed about a case of my own that had gone bad on me, and I ran against Crook in a pub—always the most likely place to meet him, unless he's in his office. 'In your shoes,' he told me, 'I'd be inclined to have a stab in the Harding affair. Very interesting. Did she do it, and if so, why?' Well, only a fool rejects Crook's advice out of hand, so I began to look into it. Odd the way straws blow in the wind. If I hadn't dropped into that bar on that particular evening, I might never have met you, my darling. You'd appreciate I'd be— concerned about the man who did that for me."

"I always wondered how Mr. Dowler got hold of you," I exploded.

"Don't underrate Dowler. You could have done a lot worse. He's a very conscientious chap."

"But not precisely a ball of fire, and that's what I needed then. Also someone who *believed* in me. I was simply his duty, and who ever gets worked up about duty?"

"Sometimes," Aubrey went on, "I wonder if a fellow like Crook hasn't got second sight. His trouble is he can't resist playing with fire. You'd think he saw himself as a giant sala-mander, impervious to the flame. Well, this should teach him different."

There was a flippant undertone to his voice now, but that didn't deceive me. He was really distressed.

Perhaps that was my opportunity, in prayer-book par-lance, to open my grief to my husband, but I didn't take it. I didn't imagine I could ever be afraid of Aubrey, but I shrank from telling him the truth now. Easier to tell him about Etta and Gerald's blackmail, only he'd wonder I hadn't broken my silence when the earring came back to me—but I couldn't ab-solve myself from responsibility. I could tell myself till I was blue in the face that this was sheer coincidence and nothing to do with me, but I saw myself standing in my little sewing room giving Mr. Crook to Gerald like something on a plate with parsley around the edge. It's guilty conscience, that's all, I told myself over and over, little rats like Gerald don't knock out Titans like Crook. Only, rats are well-known disease carriers; they can wreak as much havoc as something twenty times their size.

In my mind's eye I saw Gerald slipping in through the front door of No. 123 to lay his booby trap. The workmen would be gone before his arrival. I wondered precisely how he'd done it. Put a bit of the workmen's gear on the turn of the dark staircase, which wouldn't be seen when the light failed. Or hidden himself behind the old-fashioned curtains on the landing—the whole building had had a Victorian air and the curtains seemed *en suite*—and waited for Mr. Crook to descend. I pictured his jaunty figure tripping—the word seemed oddly appropriate despite the rotundity of his build—down the stairs, pressing the push button to light the lower staircase, finding it out of commission and—taking a chance of going down a familiar flight in the dark? Or—pushed unexpectedly as he hesitated on the top step? Even for a man who believed himself to be a descendant of the golden salamander tribe, it seemed taking an unnecessary risk.

Aubrey finished his breakfast and went off, more silent than usual, which is saying quite a lot. The post came late and there was a letter from Gavin. He seemed moderately cheerful and the expressions he employed were his own. He wanted a kite and a *large* ball of string. I read my own paper—Aubrey and I have one apiece—and got a few more details. It seemed that Mr. Crook had an arrangement with the fuzz, as he called them, that the front door of the building should be left open so long as he was himself on the premises. He kept what were discreetly referred to as unconventional hours, meaning that some of his clients found it more convenient to visit him after dark. I could almost hear him saying, "Nature knows a lot about nocturnal creatures." That pet of the nursery, Mrs.

Tiggy-Winkle, probably never went shopping till after dark. So long as there was a light in Mr. Crook's top room—the creature never seemed to have heard of curtains—the man on the beat knew that either he or Bill Parsons was still on the premises. When the light went out, the front door was closed by Mr. Crook en route for Earls Court.

The previous night the officer had noticed the door open although the upper window was dark. He had pushed the door wider and flashed on his bull's-eye, and there he lay, the King of the Bulls, dead to the world. En route to St. Edmunds by ambulance, a motley throng had risen as if from the paving stones. The rumor went around, like some invisible tom-tom: "Crook's got his. Crook's got his." Some of them followed as far as the hospital. These came surging into casualty, which, of course, was open all night, and extra police had to disperse them. "Get on home," they were told. "There's nothing you can do here." I began to understand Aubrey's expression of sympathy for the man responsible. I'd seen a little of what mob law could do after my acquittal, and that was child's play compared with this sort of mob, if the victim ever fell into their hands.

On impulse I picked up the telephone directory, but if Gerald Porter had a phone, as I was sure he had, it wasn't listed. Etta had shown common sense in operating from a different neighborhood over a different name, but it also showed that even the most cunning and the least compassionate can't win them all.

Presently, when I'd seen Aubrey go and Mrs. Day arrive, I traveled by omnibus to Bloomsbury Street. There was a policeman on guard at No. 123. I went up and said I'd had an appointment with Mr. Crook that morning—which was rather a straining of the truth—would it be possible to see Mr. Parsons instead. The policeman asked my name, then glanced at a short list he took from his pocket. Sorry, he said, my name wasn't there. These were the only people Mr. Parsons was able to see. No, he didn't think it was worth my waiting. I wasn't sure I believed in the authenticity of that list; it would be a very easy way of denying admission to curiosity-mongers and the press. The workmen were still there; if there had been any blood, it had all been polished away. To watch them going on in their leisurely but quite competent manner, you'd never guess there'd been a murder attempt on the premises a few hours before.

I turned away, and at that moment I heard steps running down the stairs, and Bill Parsons came down. He looked through me and spoke to the officer. I moved off. I wondered how often the answering phone would ring, or if it could be switched off . . . I looked over my shoulder. Bill Parsons had gone off in the opposite direction. I saw that he walked a little lame. I hadn't noticed that in the office. Later I learned that he'd been shot—though not by the police—during a gang raid in the days when he was not, in Mr. Crook's phrase, on the side of the angels. I sighed, but supposed I should have got no reason out of him today.

I walked to the end of the road and turned idly, blindly, into the next. I wondered if I should try the ansaphone for myself, but no message I could leave would be safe. The police might see the records. I wondered how badly Mr. Crook had been injured. I found I couldn't think of him as being out for the count, as he'd have put it. He was like some unwieldy phoenix that rises from its own ashes. I decided the shock had unhinged me slightly, and finding myself near a coffee shop called the Pecksniff Parlour, I drifted in and ordered a cup.

"And biscuits?" demanded the lady-in-waiting briskly.

"No biscuits."

"Biscuits are charged for, whether taken or no."

There was such an old Dickensian ring to the words that I agreed meekly I would take the biscuits. The coffee had only just arrived, and coming from a Cona, was pleasantly hot and strong, when the door opened again and a man came in and crossed at once to my table. It was Bill Parsons, and I felt so deranged it wasn't at all surprising to see him there.

"Sorry I missed you," he said. "Coffee, please."

"And biscuits?"

"If they're included. You saw about Crook," he went on as the woman, looking rather surprised, glided away.

"Of course."

"And yet you came up. And not in the hope of seeing a bloodstain. What gives?"

"I may be partly responsible—for the attack, I mean," I blurted out. "In which case, I might be able to give the man a name. Only of course I've no proof."

"Oh, we usually make our own," Bill Parsons told me.

I don't think a feature of his face moved; it was thin, aquiline, he must have been striking before his disfigurement overtook him. Now he had the look of a man who's stepped out of one world into another, and whose past bears no relation to his present. As I say, not a feature moved, yet the change that overwhelmed his face was alarming.

"The law hangs accessories before the fact the same as the actual murderers," he said.

"You mean, it used to."

"I didn't mean the Law with a capital L."

The waitress brought him coffee and biscuits. He can't really have looked as terrifying as he did to me, because she apparently noticed nothing. She could have been the unnoticing kind, but I thought you'd need to be blind not to see the implacable hate looking out from those dark, dark eyes, almost as black as coal. But not lighted, with none of coal's warming gleam. I hoped that look was for the would-be murderer, not for me.

"You were saying?" said Bill. "Drink your coffee. Or—no, that must be cold."

I picked up the cup hurriedly, saying it was quite all right, but my hand shook so that the coffee splashed into the saucer.

Bill called the waitress, told her to take it away and bring me a fresh cup.

"I saw him yesterday, Gerald Porter I mean," I explained, thinking what I really needed was about a gill of brandy, neat. "He was waiting for me when I came back from seeing Mr. Crook. I thought he was there to bend my arm, so I said I couldn't discuss anything without my lawyer's advice."

"Mention the lawyer's name?"

"That's just it," I agreed wretchedly. "I did. I thought it might make him pull in his horns a bit. Even a conceited little ape like Gerald Porter couldn't imagine himself a match for Mr. Crook."

"That's where you're wrong," said Bill. "Thank you." This to the waitress who brought the fresh coffee. "Chaps like that think themselves a match for God Almighty. Say anything special?"

"He let me know he had the earring, and later in the evening he slipped it into the letterbox in a plain envelope. My husband found it. Nothing to show where it had come from. He just said it was nice to think there were still some honest gentry going about, or something like that."

"You still haven't said why you came here today."

"I suppose I was hoping to be told I wasn't really responsible," I acknowledged, surprising myself, because I hadn't known that was the reason until this minute.

"I know Crook can do a good deal," acknowledged Bill, with a face like granite. "Leave the Miracle Boy standing at the post." (I just got the reference to Miracle Boy, a forgotten Derby runner.) "But even he can't work that sort of miracle."

"Do the police think it was a case of grievous bodily harm?" I wondered. "Or might it have been an accident."

"You don't do them justice, they're not that dumb. They know a chap like Crook doesn't lose his footing just because a light goes out."

130

"That's what my husband said. He saw it in the paper first and told me. He said he'd have a torch."

"Oh, sure," Bill agreed. "But a torch isn't much use to you when you're lying flat on your kisser at the foot of a flight of steps."

"Do you think someone could have been in hiding on the landing and given him a push." I visualized the scene so clearly, Mr. Crook pressing the light switch and no light coming on; Mr. Crook feeling for his torch and someone emerging from the dark landing to give him a flying push. He was a heavy man. Arse over tip he'd go, bump, bump down that long flight of stairs, to land among the buckets and ropes in the stone-paved hall.

"And it 'ud help if there was a handy bit of cord tied just above the second stair, say," Bill suggested.

I stared. I hadn't thought of that. "And was there?"

"With the workmen making hay all over the hall and the staircase, the police are very sensibly holding their horses, but I've noticed a small hole in the wainscot (it runs all up the staircase to the landing)—no cord there now, of course, and the paint is pretty scratched, but there it's a bit splintered."

"Did you tell them?" I asked.

"The police don't ask me for my impressions," returned Bill impassively. "Whoever the chap was, he knew what he was doing. In the ordinary way, someone hammering even a long way off will attract attention after hours, and he'd have to wait for the other officers to empty, but with workmen around, no one gives it a thought. Time and a half they get for overtime; they were working at half-six when I went out. So having fixed the cord, and given Crook all possible assistance, all X has to do is coil it up and put it in his pocket, and Bob's your uncle. If anyone sees him leave, no one's going to pay any attention. Crook's visitors are like the army of the redeemed, whom no man can number, so one rat more or less, scurrying away into the shadows, isn't going to send any good citizen scurrying to find a phone. Probably hoped no one would guess what happened before morning, and then with a bit of luck, Crook must have passed out for keeps."

"He should have shut the door," I said. "The upstairs light was out. The constable would have thought Mr. Crook had gone home."

"Except that you can't think Crook would leave the old Superb—oh, come on, Mrs. Fielding, you must have noticed that, the yellow Rolls with a bonnet as high as a duchess' eyebrows—standing unguarded by the curb all night. Crook's no great shakes on the hoof."

"It never occurred to me that Gerald Porter might try to do Mr. Crook any harm," I burst out. I sounded quite desperate.

"We don't yet know that he did." Bill seemed to have recovered his normal aplomb.

"I thought if he knew I had Mr. Crook behind me, he might think twice before doing anything melodramatic. Not that you can be much more melodramatic than pushing a man downstairs with the object of breaking his neck."

"Crook was born under the sign of the bull," Bill assured me. "Very awkward necks to break."

I came back to another problem that was troubling me. "The earring," I said.

"What about the earring?"

"Why did he give it back? It was the only hold over me he had."

"Not once he'd seen you, it wasn't. Not unless he'd already told someone he'd picked it up in Etta Cusack's room, and whoever that person was wouldn't have to believe him. I mean, he'd no proof. But now he's called at your house—a bad move that; if he'd consulted Crook, he'd have been warned never to conduct that sort of maneuver on your enemy's ground—so who's to say he didn't find it on the garden path

132

and forget to give it back to you until he'd returned to the street? No, no, Mrs. Fielding, the police would never wear that one. Before yesterday he could have taken it to them, he might even have been believed, but there'd have been nothing in it for him, and he might have been asked some rather awkward questions."

"Etta told him it was mine and that Aubrey had designed it. Doesn't that prove something?"

"Only if you have a witness. And she's underground. You could be right about last night's visitor being Gerald Porter, but again—you've no proof. Police couldn't hold him an hour on your story. Probably wouldn't even get him as far as the station. Stalemate all the way!"

"So what do we do now? Don't tell me we wait."

"What else? One thing, it's going to shake X up a lot to know he hasn't put Crook's light out after all. Oh yes, one of these days he'll have to hand in his dinner pail, but not in the middle of a case, that's not Crook's way. I'll be going round to the hospital again tonight," he added. "I don't suppose they'll object to a personal bodyguard. Hospital staffs are overworked as it is."

"Aren't you—doesn't it occur to you that having tried to shut Mr. Crook's mouth, and knowing you're in his confidence, you might be next on the list?" I burst out.

"No sense trying to nobble me till they're sure they've done for Crook," said Bill, in the voice of one to whom this is an irrelevance. "I take it you're putting your money on Gerald Porter. But there's the first husband—remember? It could be to his advantage to have Etta Cusack out of the way."

"Assuming he's married again?"

"She's got some hold over him, or why was he calling there?"

"But he can't be guilty, because I saw him leaving."

"You can't take anything for granted in this game. He could have come back; or he could have been in cahoots with the third visitor, whose identity we haven't yet established."

"Wouldn't Etta be on her guard against violence, though? I don't think it had occurred to her before that she could be threatened by one of her—creatures. You never saw anyone look so surprised as she was when she saw me with that candlestick in my hand."

"I daresay I wouldn't have felt much like St. George myself."

"So surely she'd have put it out of a visitor's reach. Gerald wouldn't count. She'd never expect him to turn."

"Yet turning worms have a long history," reflected Bill. "It's no wonder he parted with the earring. Things were getting a bit complicated. Come to that, you're not doing badly as a turning worm yourself. Mention the loss to anyone? Your husband, say."

"Not till it came back, and then he found it. Otherwise I'd just have put it back in the jewel case and said nothing."

"I've heard of some pretty chancy gamblers," Bill congratulated me. "I've always thought Crook took the bun, but you don't mind chancing your arm, do you? A husband like Aubrey Fielding, who's as much a byword in his profession as Crook is in his, and you think you can run him into the ground."

"I won't have his name mixed up in this," I cried fiercely. "He couldn't have been there that night, he was in Liverpool, and if he had been . . ."

"You'd have been dismissed as the petty cash," Bill finished brutally. "If he could have implicated Fielding, Porter would have had his hand in the mint. But even he can't hope to swing that one."

"There's still the last appointment of the day, the one after mine," I insisted.

"No proof it was ever kept. Or that whoever it was got inside the house, even if he did come."

"Mr. Fitzgerald—the one who sat with Gerald waiting

for the police—said the light was on. I suppose he could see it through the curtains. So why couldn't the visitor see it, too?"

"Oh, he could," Bill agreed. "But if you ring a bell and no one answers it, what can you do but go away? Short of smashing the window, and I don't suppose he wanted to call attention to himself, he had no choice. She doesn't seem to have operated on a very large scale," he added, switching back to Etta. "Only a few clients the police think, no names and addresses, of course, she'd have her own code. They always do. Quite safe as a rule; people who're being blackmailed are like people in chains. The knife's at your throat, what can you do but acquiesce?"

"Starting with her husband?" I wondered. "Her real husband, I mean."

"She could have blackmailed a wedding ring out of him," Bill agreed. "He went abroad after three or four years, and she didn't go with him."

"Sooner or later the luck was bound to break," I cried.

"So then you deal your last hand and make tracks for the States. Only this hand held the king of spades."

I telephoned the hospital when I got back, to get the latest news about Mr. Crook, but a male voice told me all inquiries were being blocked except for members of the family. I was tempted to say I was his married sister, but I felt quite sure Bill would have told them he hadn't a living relative. I thought of the people who must be glad he was out of the way, and wondered how long their satisfaction would last. It occurred to me that a really balanced character would find this the moment to contract out of the situation. Gerald had returned the earring, I had recovered my insane letter to Tom Cribbins, no one had identified me as the woman standing outside the door of No. 14 on the night in question, I was well and truly in the clear. I didn't imagine Bill Parsons would raise any objections. All I'd done to date was get Crook clobbered; he'd probably be glad for me to resign. Only I couldn't do it. I was too far in. Thanks to me, Crook was in hospital and his attacker might never be identified. But there must be something I could do to pay off some of my debt. It was odd how convinced I was from the start that Gerald Porter was concerned in this affair.

"We manufacture our own proof," Bill had said.

Very well, then, I would follow their example and manufacture some of my own.

10

It was a few days since I had seen Mr. James, and I hoped he might not be ill. But when I came back the following afternoon, still with no plan, he was on his familiar seat.

"A beautiful day!" I said. "I was wondering about you, hoping you weren't ill."

"There's a reason for that," said the old man. "It's not that I didn't come, but that young fellow—I can't call him a gentleman—who came the day before yesterday, well, he warned me off good and proper."

"What young fellow was that?" I asked.

"He didn't give me a name, of course, but he was wearing an Albert watch chain. It's a funny thing for a young man to be sporting, I haven't seen an Albert except on some old codger like myself these many years. Had a little metal fish dangling from it. 'What's the idea of the fish?' I said, and he told me he was born under the sign of Pisces, and honor where honor is due. Then I said if he wanted to see you, madam, I thought you were out. He said he'd wait. To tell you the truth, I didn't much like the look of him. 'Have you got permission to wait here?' I asked him. 'It's private property. It's different for me, the lady's given me permission.' 'I'm in a privileged situation,' said he, 'I don't have to ask for permission.' Well, madam, I didn't think he could be a member of your family or Mr. Fielding's, so I said you'd never mentioned to me that he might be coming, and he laughed—made me think of a hyena, honestly it did—and said something about people not wanting to wave skeletons by daylight. I did wonder if he might have stopped too long in the pub on the way, but he didn't act like a drunken man. But talking like that about skeletons—it's not as though he was a medical student. He was a young man but he was long past that. 'The right place for skeletons,' I told him, 'is in their coffins underground,' and he said but what if they had a way of breaking out every now and then. 'You a grave-digger?' I asked him, and he laughed again. I thought I should warn you, Mrs. Fielding" (he never called me that, it showed how serious he was) "that man's your enemy. He wouldn't let me stay, said you had business to discuss, and naturally I didn't want to intrude, but if there's any help I could give you . . ."

"You?" I exclaimed before I could stop myself. "Why, Mr. James, what could you do?"

"It's what I say, madam, the man's not a reliable type. Wouldn't surprise me if he was a con man or some such. Old chaps like us can always tell. Didn't grow up in any welfare state, see, so we had to stand on our own feet. One of these days you might be glad of an ally—that's what we used to call them, allies, and there's no better word—not a friend, that might be presuming . . ."

I fished for my latchkey. "I'm sorry he disturbed you," I said, "and you were in the right. You're always to come here when you want. If he comes again, don't let him drive you away. He's no right here."

Mr. James nodded his rather noble, ancient head. "Hitler had no rights in Czechoslovakia," he reminded me, "but that didn't keep him out."

"Didn't you tell me you were an old soldier?" I reproached him. I fitted my key into the lock. "I'm sure you never allowed yourself to be defeated on the field."

Mr. James drew himself up. You could almost hear the rattle of invisible medals. "I wouldn't want to take advantage," he told me.

I smiled, though my heart was heavy as lead. "You

couldn't intrude, Mr. James," I said. "And it's always a good thing to have an ally."

A day or two passed. The police didn't pay us any visits; Bill Parsons rang up to say Crook was out of his concussion, but couldn't as yet remember anything clearly. Something fell on him, he said. It could have been the Bank of England, for all he knew.

"Murder's a waiting game," he reminded me, just as Crook had done. I heard the receiver clank back onto its rest.

Meantime, I ate, slept and drank the Porter murder. There wasn't much fresh about it in the papers, but I remembered Aubrey saying that until a case was solved, the police never closed their books. They could stay open for years, then one day some fresh piece of evidence might come to light. Apart from other considerations, I knew I couldn't go on with that Damoclean sword hanging over my head. Somehow, come hell or high water, I had to *know*. It seemed to me the solution might lie with that third visitor whose identity no one had yet solved. The one person who must know, apart from the person concerned, would be Gerald. I could shut my eyes and hear Etta say, "I always let Gerald have a list—to be on the safe side," something like that. So he would know who the third person was, but he hadn't gone to the police. That could be because he didn't want to be involved in Etta's racket—she took in typing, that's what she told me, and could they prove anything different? If they could have found the tapes, or any evidence that would link him up with the blackmailing side of her job, surely they'd have moved by now. Here it occurred to me that Gerald might be carrying on where Etta had been compelled to leave off. He should be on pretty safe ground; the victims wouldn't want publicity. I was less sorry for them now than I'd been at the start, they were paying for their own folly or carelessness. If they hadn't been stupid, as I'd been stupid, they could never have been in her power at all.

I hadn't an address for Gerald and he wasn't listed in the telephone book, but I remembered Etta telling me they had a very comfortable and modern flat in the most recently built block near the zoo, so all I had to do was go to Regents Park and find out the name of the newest building. Once I'd found that, I could ring any bell, ask for Mr. Porter and then apologize because I'd got the wrong number. Sooner or later someone would tell me the right one.

I had no fixed plan of campaign when I left the house. I just saw one step ahead, and my first step was to discover his whereabouts. The newest block I could find wasn't one of these tall chimneypot affairs, but a rather low architectural development that toned very well with the actual zoo. There were four entrances, and at each, a set of buzzers, like the flats in a private house. I suppose it saved visitors the trouble of taking the lift up, and gave the tenants some chance of knowing who was calling. Against flat No. 46 was the name Mr. & Mrs. G. Porter. My first step was achieved. Unless Gerald suddenly materialized and realized I was snooping, this wasn't a particularly dangerous development for me. The next would be much more perilous, and I couldn't think of any allies to call on, not unless I could mysteriously stumble on some fresh clue or throw up some suggestion that could command official respect. I turned away from the flats and went into the park.

The glorious weather had continued. There were children on the lake driving little boats around, ducks were diving and swimming and having mock battles or suddenly taking wing and going in formations of five or six against that glittering sky. The trees were a brilliant green, and I found myself remembering W. F. Harvey's poem: *From troubles of the world I turn to ducks.*

Only, I reminded myself, I couldn't stand mooning about, enjoying the kind of ballet they made with the other waterfowl, I'd got to make some plan. I started to walk slowly around the lake, noticing no one. Somewhere the answer to the puzzle lay concealed. There's always an answer, Aubrey used to say; it's up to us to find it. Sometimes no one did and the case went down as an unsolved crime. But not this one, I told myself furiously, not this one.

He also said you had to have respect for the law, and I realized that this was a disadvantage he shared with the police. Mr. Crook didn't care a hoot about the law. Wrastle, gouge and rabbit-punch, he'd said, and the Last Trump would find him wrastling and gouging undeterred. It occurred to me I didn't have to have any special respect for the law either. I only had to play it clever. I hadn't shown any particular intelligence so far, but this was a new chapter. I'd cheat my own guardian angel if I had to. All I had to do was think up a fool-proof plan to make Gerald betray himself—or that third visitor whom obviously he was shielding for his own interests. It occurred to me that most often in murder mysteries the difficulty is to identify the criminal. I used to wonder at those country-house murders, where about fourteen people are invited for the weekend and about thirteen of them have excellent motives for wanting their host out of the way. It must have been a blow to their authors when country-house life went out of fashion. This situation was different. I was sure I could finger the criminal, but I didn't know how to prove it. I hadn't even got a definite motive, though I could think of half a dozen reasons why Gerald should want Etta out of the way.

A white duck came marching toward me, as stately as Queen Victoria, and in sidestepping her, I nearly fell into the pond. A park official appeared out of the ground to say sternly, "That's no way for a grown person to carry on. You have to think of the ducks. If you was to fall in here, they could suffer a big shock, and this is no time of year for shocks."

"I slipped," I defended myself.

But he wasn't pacified. "Plenty of room for everyone. You don't have to walk on the rim."

A small covey of ducks sailed by, making a good deal of noise. Laughing, perhaps?

The chiming of a nearby clock saved me. I counted the notes in amazement. I looked unbelievingly at my watch. It didn't seem possible that I had been drifting around the lake for so long and have made virtually no headway. Aubrey had anticipated a hard day, and would be home about eight. He wouldn't want to go out again, and I had told Mrs. Day I would bring back food for our dinner. Fortunately, this was the evening when some of the Sloane Square neighborhood shops stayed open till seven.

I hurried back to the main road and picked up a taxi, which drove me to Hambridges, the new all-embracing store (largely backed by dollars, someone said) near Sloane Square. I bought smoked salmon and escaloppe and a special sort of Bavarian cheese that Aubrey liked and a pineapple. The pineapple was rank extravagance. Then I remembered I'd promised to pick up a new transistor for his radiogram—he didn't care much about television but he listened in a good deal. I was paying for the transistor when someone called my name quite desperately, and there was Connie Winchester, a crazy friend of Aubrey's and mine, married to a tycoon and getting as much fun out of spending his money as a child turned loose in a five-and-ten store with a fifty-penny piece.

"Just the person I wanted to see," she panted. She looked rather like a Victorian milkmaid, pink cheeks and fair hair and one of those big floppy hats that were being worn just then, that partially concealed her face.

As always, she bubbled with enthusiasm. I tried to explain I had to get back for Aubrey's dinner, but she paid no attention at all. "He won't mind if you're a few minutes late. He can have another drink. And I need you, Meg."

She was always like that, would never have believed that anyone else's interest could possibly be greater than her own.

She ought to have been a thorn in the sides of shop assistants, she changed her mind so frequently and bewilderingly, sometimes even when the parcel was being wrapped, but somehow they always brightened up at the sight of her. She might give a lot of trouble— But why not, darling? she would urge. It's what they're paid for—but she streaked through department after department like some glittering bird. "I'm trying to get something for Henry's birthday," she cried in her high, fluting voice. "He's mad about electrical gadgets. I did think of an electric toothbrush . . ."

"You mean, he hasn't got one yet?"

"He never *gets* himself anything, he just loves to *have* it. Only he's so over the moon thinking about something else most of the time, he'd probably electrocute himself. All electric gadgets have their dangerous side."

"We sell a great many for children," put in the shop assistant.

"Ah, but they have mothers and nurses to supervise them. You can't supervise a man of forty-four. There was this stereo . . ."

"You can't do anything with that but turn it on and off," I pointed out. "Anyway, a thing that size would need a room to itself."

"It 'ud need a house to itself the way Henry would play it." She shuddered. "Oh, look." She indicated a weird contraption for washing the car electrically.

"Doesn't the garage do that for him?" I said.

"What a wet blanket you are, Meg. He always says they never get the mud from under the mudguards, and this has got a special attachment—Look, I really do believe he would like this. It doesn't mean he couldn't go on sending the car to the garage, but he'd so enjoy *playing* with it, and that's the whole point of a present."

The assistant hastened to exploit its virtues. I wondered

why it wasn't in the automobile department before it occurred to me that perhaps cars were among the few things they didn't sell.

"I do so hate these messy buckets and cloths and polishers all over the pavement at weekends," Connie went on. "And Henry would really feel he'd done a man's job if he cleaned his own car better than the garage did."

She could be right at that, I thought. Rich men are often taken that way. "And when he wasn't using it you could have it for yours," I suggested.

"Oh no," said Connie decidedly. "Henry wouldn't like that. He's very generous but he does like his things to be *his*. He won't even share a tube of toothpaste. I believe he'd buy me a second car-cleaner sooner than share this one."

While she gave her name and address and insisted on making out a check—it couldn't go on the general list, she explained, because this was a present—I wandered on around the department. I have a secret yearning after electrical gadgets myself. Beyond the wireless department the store was showing an exhibition of mini pocket tape recorders, just over from the States. They came in various sizes and shapes. Suddenly I stood frozen, like Lot's wife when she looked over her shoulder and was turned into the pillar of salt. One of the mini recorders was shaped like a watch, one of the old-fashioned turnip watches men used to wear. Mr. Crook had one still, I'd seen him pull it out and consult it.

This, then, I thought, was the explanation of Gerald's ridiculous Albert chain. I reflected I'd never seen him draw the watch from his pocket, and surely if he wanted some means of identification, he could have chosen something a little less conspicuous. It explained so much else, too. Why had Gerald been at the Teapot and Dormouse on that first occasion? Surely not just to collect the drinks. And I recalled that Etta hadn't said anything that really bore on the situation until he had rejoined us. The cunning both had displayed made me blind with anger. What use was there in buying back the incriminating evidence when the record stood in another form? It was the same kind of rage that had led me to destroy the tape recorder in Klondyke Street. I thought if Gerald were suddenly to emerge here, I might try to destroy him, too.

Slowly recovering myself, I started to walk on; the recorders came in various shapes. I thought you could hardly give a small boy a greater treat than bring him here—except that it would break his heart not to be allowed to take one back with him. I kept seeing memories rush across the front of my mind like great leaves blown off trees. Gerald in the garden of our house and subsequently in my sewing room. What precisely had I said? I'd acknowledged the existence of the earring, I had spoken freely of my visit to Etta—what else had I said? Enough to put me back in Queer Street, I was certain of that. And I'd been telling myself complacently that now was the time to pull out if I wanted to. Pull out? I was in it up to the neck.

I only remembered Connie several minutes later when I heard her unmistakable voice fluting about my friend . . . not deserted me. I went rather dazedly to meet her.

"Oh, there you are," she said. "Henry will be worried about my being so late. What on earth have you been doing, darling? I thought you were here to help me buy Henry's present."

When we reached the lift I found I'd left my dinner parcels behind, so I told Connie to go on while I fetched them.

"I'd wait for you," said Connie earnestly, "really I would. But I have to think of Henry, don't I?"

I went back and found my parcels. It was getting quite late—we must have lingered a long time in Hambridges— when I came onto the pavement. A taxi was going past and I flagged it. Aubrey had said he wouldn't be back before eight, but when I got out of the cab I saw there were lights burning in the house. I blessed my good luck that I'd met Connie. She was my perfect alibi.

I went into the house calling Aubrey's name. I'd hoped to be back first and have a word with Bill Parsons while I had the house to myself. I wanted to tell him what I'd discovered and what I proposed to do about it. I had my plan cut if not altogether dried. Now I must take my chance of getting to the telephone while Aubrey's attention was distracted. I opened the door, but it wasn't my husband who came to meet me, but Mrs. Day, looking very pale and stern.

"I was afraid you might have met with an accident, too," she said.

"Too? What is it? Mr. Fielding . . ."

"No, madam, it's not quite so bad as that."

Like Mr. James, she would call me madam, which I didn't much care for. I never could see why I should be given a title that smacks of obsequiousness, which I've done nothing to deserve. "But—your old gentleman, Mr. James . . . Oh, it's a shame, madam, a nice old man like that. No trouble to anyone and never presumed. If I was to take him out a cup of tea from the kitchen pot he'd never take it for granted, not like some."

"Mrs. Day," I said, thinking I must be screaming, but her face didn't change, so presumably I sounded reasonably controlled. "What has happened to Mr. James?"

"He's met with an accident, madam. All along of that man."

"Which man was that?"

"He wasn't a gentleman," declared Mrs. Day, and I heard the echo of Mr. James' voice. "You couldn't call him a gentleman, madam. A common type, I'd say. Mr. James may not have had much in the way of money or position, but his heart was right. This one pushed open the gate and marched into the garden as if he owned it. I happened to be at the window. I was just thinking I'd take a cup of tea to the old gentleman—

146

we used to sit together on the seat sometimes in nice weather and sup it, quite domesticated it made me feel. When I was a girl I used to think when I was too old to work . . ." She caught sight of my face and broke off. "Like I said, madam, he was walking up the path as free as you please, and Mr. James, he stood up and told him off. 'I've warned you before,' I heard him say—though, to be honest with you, madam, I'd never seen him before. I opened the window an inch or two, but I couldn't really hear, just something about not needing permission, that was the intruder"—she gave the word an emphasis an actress might have envied—"and then I distinctly heard Mr. James say something about the police. The other one said, 'You wouldn't dare!' Well, madam, you know that's not the kind of thing you can say to an old gentleman like Mr. James. He turned straight away and made for the gate.

"I wanted to call through the window not to trust him. (He's unreliable, Mr. James had said. You can always tell.) But they'd gone. And then a minute or two later there was this terrible commotion and I ran to the gate. It's amazing, madam, how a street can be empty one minute, and the next as full of people as if they'd flown out of trees. I didn't go down, of course, I'm against crowds on principle. Anyway, I knew if I waited someone would tell me what had happened. And sure enough, a woman came rushing past, waving her hands and saying wasn't it a terrible thing, didn't *I* think it was a terrible thing? But I didn't know what had happened and so I said, and she told me an old gentleman had slipped on the curb and fallen right under a car. Well, madam, I could see at once what had happened, the little chap had pushed the old gentleman under the car. I daresay Mr. James knew something. My husband used to say you can learn more at a place like the Fig and Thistle than you could in the Houses of Parliament, and who's to say he's not right? Well, madam, it must have been something like that. Fancy him trailing Mr. James all the way here, and then trying to drive him out."

"You'd never seen him before, you said?"

"It's not likely he'd have come a second time if I had, madam."

To do her justice, I thought she was probably right, and she wouldn't even have had to hoist a rolling pin. Gerald would have gone. Don't ask me how I could be so sure. I just knew. The forces of righteousness, perhaps, and in the circumstances, I could hardly expect to have them on my side. Still, I reminded myself, I had Mr. Crook until Gerald scored there, too. Perhaps Etta had known what she was doing when she teamed up with him. He was as unscrupulous as herself.

"Anyway," Mrs. Day went on, "I asked this woman if Mr. James had been alone, and she said there was someone—she couldn't describe him—near by who tried to help him, but it was no good. If you want my opinion, madam, I don't believe it was an accident at all. I've seen Mr. James in the street, very careful he always was, looked both ways before crossing a road, never ran up against a tree or slipped in a dog's mess. Is it likely, I ask you, madam, he'd fall off a curb just when a car was going by?"

"What was he like—this other man?" I asked her.

"Since you ask me, madam, he looked like everybody else—only there was one thing, he was wearing one of these Albert watch chains, which you don't often see these days. Apart from that, well, I might recognize him, and again I might not. I didn't see him so clearly, you understand. Only— why did he follow Mr. James down here? Not for money, we all know Mr. James hadn't much of that. No, he knew something about him, Mr. James did, and he was going to the police."

"Have you said anything about this to anyone?" I asked.

"I don't like to mix with just anyone," said Mrs. Day. "Mr. Day was the same. And of course I didn't actually *see* what happened, it's just that I know."

148

"Did you hear how badly hurt he was?"

Mrs. Day stared at me in amazement. "Well, madam, is it likely a big car—a ton and more some of them weigh—could go over an old gentleman and just break his leg? Oh, they had the police and the ambulance, I heard the bells, and people talked, but you'll see, when it comes to the crunch, no one will remember or say much . . ."

"I wonder if he had any family."

"He lost a son in the North Sea in the last war, that I do know. Never spoke of grandchildren, and he'd been a widower this many a year. Spoke very well of the woman in whose house he lodged—well, madam, no, I don't know just where it was, but not far off, I'd say—still, that's not like having a home, is it?"

"No brothers or sisters?"

"He never said. Come to that, they'd be pretty old, too. Or it could be he didn't keep in touch. Families do drift. Not that he talked much about himself, as decent an old gentleman as you could look for. He deserved to die in his bed, like any Christian should."

"I wonder where they took him."

"It 'ud be St. Richard, that's the nearest. They'd keep him in the mortuary till he was identified. I wouldn't have liked a stranger identifying Mr. Day, but you have to make the best of what you've got, don't you, madam?"

Later that evening I rang the hospital, giving my name and asking about the old man. I explained elliptically that he used to come into our garden. He had only just left us, I said, when the disaster occurred.

I was passed on to someone else, who told me Mr. James had been dead on arrival; death must have been practically instantaneous. This, I think, was intended as consolation. The speaker then asked if I knew the names of any relatives who should be notified, someone who could identify the body.

"I never understood that he had any family," I said. "There were his lodgings." But I couldn't even supply the address of those.

The voice turned crusty. "I thought you said he was your gardener."

"Not precisely," I acknowledged. "He used to sit in our garden sometimes." I added very reluctantly that if there was no one else to identify him, I could do it. I would wait, I said, until my husband came back and we could come down together. I left my name and telephone number. Kind Mrs. Day brought me some tea, though I felt what I really needed was about a gill of brandy.

"I'm sure," she said, "if I look out of my window on a sunny day, I'll never find that seat empty. There'll always be a ghost there . . ."

I saw that for all the kindness of her heart, she was beginning to relish the tragedy in a macabre sort of way. I suppose really that is the best way to treat it.

When I heard the door close behind her I thought of all the people who complain of life's monotony. I could do with a bit of blessed monotony myself just now, I decided. I hoped Aubrey wouldn't mind coming down to the mortuary later on; I didn't feel I could face the ordeal alone. He had never met the old man, so far as I knew, but he'd often heard me speak of him. It wouldn't occur to him that it wasn't an accident, but for myself I had no doubts at all. He had been a very sincere old chap; if he said he was going to the police, then he meant what he said. And doubtless it wouldn't be convenient for Gerald if the old man started to stir up trouble. He'd have to explain what he was doing in the garden anyway, and he wouldn't want to do that.

And so poor Mr. James had to die. I don't think the prospect would trouble Gerald at all. You tread on a cockroach, catch a mouse in a trap. Vermin can't be allowed to proliferate. Mr. James would approximate to the mouse or the beetle in

150

Gerald's view. And it was all for nothing. Mr. James couldn't have done him any harm. It's no crime to walk into someone else's garden, presumably to ring the bell. But none of us as yet could be sure in which direction police suspicions were pointing. So far they'd made no move toward arresting anyone. Aubrey would say reasonably, "How can they? They're waiting for proof." Mr. Crook would say, "Trust the fuzz not to chance its arm."

As soon as Aubrey came in he realized something was wrong. When I told him about Mr. James, he said, "Poor old chap! London roads are a death trap to the aged."

"He was quite spry," I objected.

"But not spry enough. You weren't there, I hope?"

"Mrs. Day got the news from a passer-by who saw it happen. She waited—Mrs. Day, that is—for me to come back. I ran into Connie Winchester . . ."

"In that case, it's greatly to your credit that you came home at all," said Aubrey smoothly.

"I rang the hospital," I went on. "They suggested I should go down and identify him. He doesn't seem to have had any relations."

But in the end we didn't, because Mr. James' landlady got worried when he didn't come back to his supper, and reported him to the police, and was told what had happened. She'd been to the Bottle and Jug, where he might be lingering, but no one had seen him that evening, so she knew something was wrong. We heard that a woman in the street had reported that she'd seen the accident, only she wasn't so sure it had been one, if they understood what she meant. There'd been a man walking beside him, and she thought he'd given the old boy a push, either to get him out of the way because he didn't move fast enough or just out of sheer spite. She wasn't suggesting that the man in question had deliberately pushed Mr. James under a car. I was now concerned for Mrs. Day. If Gerald had seen her or thought she might recognize him, her life might be in jeopardy, too. The one person I could have talked to about this was Mr. Crook, and he was out of circulation. I couldn't even at that stage confide in Aubrey.

The day seemed to have been broken clean in half. I dutifully cooked the escaloppe, but it might have been corn flakes, for all the taste it had for me. It wasn't till we were getting ready for bed that I remembered my plans for the morrow and my intention to give Bill Parsons warning of what I had in mind. It was too late to do anything now, I'd have to make the call first thing in the morning.

11

Next morning Aubrey was on the telephone even before breakfast. At ten o'clock it was obvious he wasn't going to leave for his office yet, so I resolved to do my phoning from a public call box. I waited for Mrs. Day, because I particularly wanted to know if Gerald had had a good look at her.

"I should hope not, madam," she said. "But that doesn't mean I didn't see him. And I shall always believe he was responsible for Mr. James going under that car."

"The police won't accept that as proof," I said, and she looked shocked.

"I hope it's not coming to the police, madam. Mr. Day wouldn't have liked that at all. Decent honest people don't have to be concerned with them, they're there for the criminal classes. Once you get mixed up with the police, Mr. Day used to say, before you know where you are, you're telling them things you didn't know you knew, and as like as not they're calling you a liar because you hadn't known you knew them."

"Mr. Fielding's still here," I said. "I have to go out." I put my head around the corner of his study door. "I'll be back to lunch," I told him.

"You won't find me here," Aubrey promised. "Well, have a good hair-do or whatever." He spoke like a man in a fog. Before I'd slammed the front door he'd pro tem forgotten my existence.

I tried the phone at the end of the road, but the box was occupied by someone who seemed blissfully prepared to spend half the morning there. Through the window I could see a small pile of coins ready to be slipped into the slot. Old Dan Cupid, I wondered? Or someone trying to find accommodation at short notice? The next telephone had been wrecked by vandals. After that I sighted my bus, which didn't run very often, so I decided to try my luck at the other end.

The bus put me down at Primrose Hill, wreathed in sunlight. There were children playing around the hawthorn trees that flowered in a glory of rose and snow. Near the zoo I found an empty box and rang Crook's number, but once again I got only the familiar impersonal voice asking me to leave a message, giving my name, address and telephone number. I wondered if Bill was at the hospital. (I learned afterward that he had had all incoming calls transferred to the ansaphone. Crook's clients would keep telephoning to know when he'd be back on the job. Their first sympathy had withered, now they were beginning to feel affronted that he should be neglecting their interests for so long.)

When I reached Goodwood Mansions a taxi had drawn up in front of the entrance I proposed to use, and the driver and commissionaire, a man with a thin sly aggressive face, the type that knows the whole world is his enemy, were unloading a mountain of luggage. I didn't want to attract attention and I also wanted to give Bill a chance to see my message; anyway, there'd be no room in the lift with the immense lady who surged out of the taxi, as vindictive in her way as the commissionaire, so I crossed the road and sat on a seat the authorities had thoughtfully provided. I felt I appreciated old Mr. James' relief at finding somewhere to sit, and remembering him and what had happened—the inquest was to be this afternoon—all my rage boiled up again. I remembered an old woman I'd once met on another London bench. She said she came from Aldgate, where they used to have seats in the churchyard. So companionable, she said. You could get into conversation with anyone who came along, and if nobody did, there was always something to be seen on the graves, an unusual inscription or a telling memorial.

I was still thinking about her when a man, with the air of one to whom time is of no importance, sauntered down the road and dropped into the corner at the other end of the seat. He wore a gay checked coat that matched the day, and settled at once to a crossword. The sun blazed, the clouds were like alabaster against that blue china sky. I glanced at my companion. He gave the impression of a man utterly at peace; he didn't even seem to realize my existence. I found myself envying that tranquil carefree outlook, though he hardly looked like one of the successful throng. Most likely he knew it and it didn't bother him a bit. At the flats the commotion was dying down, the taxi had driven off, the imposing lady and her luggage had disappeared. I couldn't see the commissionaire, gone for a delayed coffee break perhaps. This might be my chance.

I stood up, then turned to my companion. "Excuse me," I said. "Will you be here for the next twenty minutes or so?"

He scarcely turned his head. "What's that to you, lady? Seats are free for all, aren't they?"

"Well, of course they are," I said. "It's just—I have to visit one of those flats opposite, and if I'm not down in twenty minutes, would you call the police?"

He said something about a right nutter and I muttered something about my husband. I put my hand in my coat pocket.

"What have you got there?" he demanded suspiciously.

"I'm not armed," I said. "This isn't melodrama." Then it occurred to me that was exactly what it was. "I can't explain," I said. "Only if I'm not down . . ."

The opposite doorway was clear and there was no traffic to impede my crossing.

"Shouldn't you take a rozzer with you, dear?" the man said.

"Oh no," I assured him sincerely. "That wouldn't be a good idea at all." I frowned. "My husband . . ." I began.

He shrugged. "Please yourself," he said.

He went back to his crossword. Perhaps he was accustomed to being approached by solitary females making outrageous requests. It had just occurred to me that if I had someone holding a watching brief, it might make my situation a little more secure. Gerald was no angel; if he hadn't any scruple about pushing an old man under a car, he wouldn't make much more of shoving me out of a window. The flats had large picture windows, very convenient for would-be murderers.

As I walked through the door of the flats, the lift whined to a halt and two men got out. One was a big extrovert type, the other the commissionaire-porter carrying two air suitcases. These he set on the floor. "I'll nip along to the corner," he said. "Shan't be a jiff. There's usually a cruiser at this time of day."

I thought he'd be lucky. I hadn't seen an empty taxi since my arrival. I wondered if he'd noticed me sitting on the seat opposite, but if he had, he gave no sign. I paused by the doorway; iron railings controlled some shrubs and plants. I drooled over a magnolia that was just opening its great waxen blooms to the light. The porter didn't even notice me. Women staring at flowers in London come a dime a dozen. It's odd, really, more women aren't used for private investigation work. They could go anywhere and no one would notice them.

The commissionaire hurried off and I moved into the hall. The extrovert traveler stood like a statue, not aware of anyone but himself. I moved to the lift and pressed the button. Nothing happened, of course, because the lift was already at the ground floor. Looking over my shoulder, I saw the man who had shared my seat fold his paper small and put it in his pocket. Then he got up and slouched off. Someone else who didn't want to be involved, I thought scornfully. But then I thought he showed his good sense, not wanting to tangle with a woman who was having husband trouble. I couldn't think why I'd mentioned Aubrey. Anyway, I was on my own now.

I was still standing by the lift trying to figure exactly what I was going to say when a voice in my ear observed, "It's not an automatically opening lift. And there's no attendant, if that's what you were waiting for."

I muttered something incoherent and pulled at the lift gate. "I was wondering which floor No. 46 was on," I said. It occurred to me there couldn't be too many people knowing whither I was bound.

"Fourth floor," said the extrovert, and then the commissionaire came bustling in with the air of a man who's actually built the taxi himself.

I got into the lift and rode up to the fourth floor. There were four flats on each floor; No. 46 was opposite the lift gate. But when I rang the bell, no one answered. I don't know why it had never occurred to me that Gerald might be out; in my rage I decided to stay, leaning against the door till his return. I rang again, long and furiously, and now I heard steps within. The door opened a few inches, and there he was, the mousy little man still wearing his Albert watch chain. When he saw me he looked as though he'd have closed the door in my face, but I was too quick for him.

"Am I late?" I asked quickly. "I make it almost eleven."

He didn't pull out his watch, which would have been an automatic reaction. Instead he asked, "What's so sacred cow about eleven?"

"You mean, you weren't expecting me?"

"Your letter must have gone astray."

"I'd like a word with you about Mr. James," I said.

"Mr.—?"

"You don't have to play it so dumb," I told him. "You were seen in our garden yesterday afternoon. Someone remembered your watch chain."

"So?"

157

"Mr. James was killed by a car last night."

"These old chaps shouldn't go around alone," said Gerald easily.

"That's the point. He wasn't alone. A woman in the crowd saw you together . . ."

"You're married to a lawyer," said Gerald. "Haven't you learned from him that you can't come round making accusations, because that's what it amounts to. I don't know anything about your old soldier . . ."

"I didn't say he was a soldier."

"You made him sound like one."

"Aren't you going to ask me in," I added, raising my voice as a woman came out of an adjacent flat, "or is this an inconvenient time?"

"I've got a man here on business," Gerald said.

The woman pottered along the passage as if she wondered what she'd left undone at home—left the gas on or the saucepan boiling.

"I have to see you," I said quite desperately. "The police . . ."

The woman pricked up her ears, and Gerald muttered something. "You'd better come in, I suppose, but make it short. I'm telling you the truth when I say I've got someone here."

As he closed the front door, the door of what was presumably the living room opened a crack. So he was telling the truth when he said he wasn't alone in the flat. The next instant I'd gone rigid. You hear about people coming back from the dead—ghosts, phantoms, weird messages. The voice I heard now was the voice of someone who had gone to her grave a while ago.

"No sense spoiling the ship for a ha'porth of tar," said Etta's unmistakable voice. "And what I'm asking's only a flea-bite to Ed Lambourn's daughter."

"Who's that?" I cried, and the door opened wider and a

158

man stood on the threshold. I recognized him at once, though it was clear he didn't know me. We'd met once before on the doorstep of 14 Klondyke Street. "Mr. Tracy!" I said before anyone could speak. And I turned back to Gerald. "So you are carrying on—I wondered."

The two voices, reproduced on the tape, paid no attention to us.

"He thought you were dead," insisted a voice I'd never heard before. I put my hands in my pockets; it seemed the wisest thing to do. "He couldn't know you'd changed your name."

"Too mean to pay for a copy of the certificate," said Etta, and I could swear she was laughing. "He only had to get in touch with Somerset House. All deaths are recorded there, and anybody can apply for a copy of the death certificate, but it does cost a little."

"He believed you were dead," insisted the voice more passionately than before. "Would he have married me if he'd known he still had a wife living?"

"He'd have been a fool to pass up Ed Lambourn's daughter. What is it you inherit—next year, isn't it? Half a million dollars. It only surprises me he didn't forge the death certificate. But perhaps he did. Forging's his thing, you know. Or didn't he tell you? Wives can't give evidence against their husbands, or he might have got five years."

"I don't know who you are or why you're butting in here," said Tracy whitely. "Is this another of your tricks, Porter?"

"She could go jump in the pond for me," returned Gerald elegantly, "but she's not the obliging kind. Here, turn that thing off." He moved forward and stopped the tape recorder. "I told you I was engaged," he added to me.

"I've wondered a lot about you since Etta's death," I said to Tracy. "You don't remember a woman coming to the door about six-thirty that night and asking for Mrs. Cusack?"

He hesitated, and I went on, "No need to be shy about it. It was a piece of cake for you that I turned up, because I'm the one person who knows she was alive after you'd gone—me and the murderer, of course."

"Why are you here?" he demanded.

"She's here because she realizes she's the last person who admits to seeing my wife alive." This, of course, was Gerald.

"I thought Etta was Mr. Tracy's wife," I said unpardonably. "What did Etta mean about forging being your thing? Is that why you married her?"

"I married her because that's what she wanted," said Tracy. "Well, she might get a ring out of me but she couldn't make me stay the course."

"Did you really think she was dead when you married Ed Lambourn's daughter? Oh!" I was shocked at my own slowness to catch on. "That's her Etta was talking to. Oh, how pleased Etta must have been to think she was double-crossing you both. So she came to Klondyke Street." I stopped again. "Was she the third visitor?" Things were beginning to fall into place so rapidly I felt a bit dazed. "Does she wear Miss Rayne shoes?" I asked. "And a broad-brimmed black hat? So she was there that night . . ."

"She didn't get in," shouted Tracy. "She knows nothing about Etta's death. She didn't get in."

Gerald stepped forward and put the tape machine in motion again. "The tape recorder, like the camera, cannot lie," he said.

"Don't let him fool you," I told Tracy. "Even if she got in that night, there couldn't have been any record made, because the machine was smashed. I smashed it myself."

"She was seen at the door," Gerald said.

And another piece of the puzzle slid into place. I'd been a bit worried about the woman who had, as I supposed, told the police she had seen me standing on the step about seven P.M., because there hadn't been any lights in any of the houses oppo-

160

site, I had been certain of that. But, of course, it wasn't me she had seen. And the girl—I should have known that you don't go to meet your lover in Euston wearing those clothes—she hadn't been immersed in love's young dream, she'd glimpsed me on the step and gone into her act immediately. One thing about Etta, she'd taught us all to be good actresses. I winced at the thought of myself deceiving Aubrey, whom I dearly loved. I tried to console myself with the thought that I'd never actually told him a lie, but I couldn't fool myself. Lies are in the soul, rather than on the lips. She'd gone into the café-tabac, this girl who could feel Etta's hot breath on her neck—half a million dollars, had that been the sum?—because she couldn't hang about the streets and there was nowhere else for her to go.

"I saw her," I said. "Only I didn't guess. I saw you, too," I added to Gerald. "You were hiding in the little alley beyond the newspaper stand."

"You don't miss much, do you?" said Gerald. He was still as smooth as cream. "So now you can understand why I'm so sure that she did get in."

"You mean, you saw her?"

"That's what I mean."

"But she must have been all right after that," I urged, "because you talked to her. She told you about the earring."

"What earring was that?" asked Gerald.

"The one you brought back to my house. My husband found it in the letterbox."

"I don't know what you're talking about," Gerald said. "I didn't see Etta that evening till I came round and found her dead."

"Because she hadn't come back at eight as she'd promised. When did she promise?"

"She told me that morning, of course. It would save us all time if you were to tell me why you're here."

I looked at Tracy. "Who's Ed Lambourn?"

Tracy stared.

Gerald said, "First cousin to Onassis. She brought quite a sizable fortune to her husband—only poor girl"—he was talking about the one who went by the name of Mrs. Tracy—"she had no husband."

"She can marry him now," I said. Something was bugging me. I was keeping the conversation going till I discovered what it was. Crook—no, it was Bill Parsons—had been right when he said the earring was no longer any use as a blackmail weapon to Gerald Porter. Gerald himself had the wit to see that, so he had neatly got himself out from under. But I still had no doubt in my mind that it was he who had killed Etta. To say nothing of trying to kill Crook and successfully pushing old Mr. James under a car. I had no hope of proving either of the last two, but every criminal puts a foot wrong sooner or later, I had heard Crook say so.

"Why did you go round to Klondyke Street instead of just ringing up?" I asked.

"I did ring, but there was no reply."

"You might have thought she'd started home."

"I waited till eight-thirty."

"And then you came round and—of course you had your own key."

"Naturally."

"So you went in, and there she was. So what did you do?"

"I rang the police. Then as I came out of her room I met this fellow, Fitzgerald, in the hall, and he sat with me till they arrived."

"And you just picked up the earring by chance and knew it was mine?"

"I've told you, I know nothing about an earring." He smiled, a puffy, sneering sort of smile. "Anything else you'd like to know?"

"Yes," I said, "I'd like to know how you rang the police

on a phone that was out of order. I fell over it and broke it on my way out."

"I rang from the telephone booth in the alley."

"The one you tried to ring from before, when I saw you disappearing down there?"

Tracy broke in, "You mean, you were there that evening?"

"I repeat," said Gerald, taking no notice of the question, "that I telephoned to the police from the telephone booth in the alley."

"But you said just now that you came round and found her and as you came out of the room you ran into Mr. Fitzgerald and you stayed together till the police arrived. You can't have rung from her phone, because it was out of order, so if you rang from the alley, it must have been before you came into the house. Which means, you knew you were going to need them. And how did you know if you hadn't been on the premises?"

"I came to No. 14, I found her, I went out to telephone, I came back and met Fitzgerald in the hall and we waited together."

"That's not what you said just now. You said you came out of her room and ran into Fitzgerald in the hall. You told him what had happened, and he sat with you till the police came." I turned to Tracy. "Isn't that so?"

"Perhaps," remarked Gerald airily to Tracy, "I should take that record to the police." He nodded toward the recorder. "Duty of a citizen, and so forth."

"You can't do that," said Tracy sharply. He turned to me. "I think you have become a bit confused. Porter never said he'd telephoned from his wife's room. You've got the wrong impression."

His face was gray with anxiety. He wasn't a bad-looking man, but I could see how Etta could have twisted him around her little finger. Forgery's his thing, she'd said. So she'd caught him out in some felony and made marriage the price of her silence. I wondered why she'd wanted him particularly—it didn't occur to me she might have been in love with him—then I remembered that in some small community he was quite someone, while her prospects weren't very bright. She could go on for years as social secretary to one hotel after another. As a married woman with her own establishment, and local connections, she'd be in a far stronger position. If I hadn't known her so well I might have been sorry for her, but I remembered her lying her head off to get me convicted just to save herself from a barely probable suspicion. I wondered about her other victims. How many of them hadn't been able to stand the pace? Only in law that's no murder. Anyway, I supposed we'd never know.

"Don't let him fool you," I warned Tracy. "He can demand a small fortune for that record, but that wouldn't be the end of the story. He's been just as skillful double-crossing you as ever Etta was. Ask him to tell you the time by that lovely watch he wears on a chain."

I had run out of discretion long ago, was well in the red, but now even I could see I'd gone too far. Gerald's face reminded me of a Chinese mask I'd once seen of a tiger showing its fangs. Any second now, I thought, and they'll be sunk in my throat. But still I couldn't let well alone. "If you want to know the time, ask a policeman," I gibed.

Tracy turned toward Gerald. His face was a study. "What's she talking about, Porter? All this about a watch?"

"I don't think she knows herself," said Gerald. "All the same, I'm not sure she should be allowed to go round making trouble for us. I warned you before," he added to me, "to keep a guard on that tongue of yours. But you won't be told, will you?"

"She doesn't know anything," Tracy said defensively.

"She knows much too much, and what's more, she knows how to dress it up. And if you're prepared to take the risk, I'm not."

I wondered what on earth he meant by that. In films wicked men suddenly produced hypodermic needles and stabbed victims with deadly drugs; or they broke their necks by karate, but I didn't think Gerald could have anything of that sort in mind. It would be too difficult for him to explain away the corpse. It was going to be a nuisance, though, if I had to be on guard every time I crossed a road. I thought of Mr. James again, though he, of course, hadn't been on guard.

"You want to be careful," muttered Tracy, who hadn't even the courage of a bad man.

"And that's a piece of advice you might take to heart," I agreed. "If I'm not out of this flat in one piece twenty minutes after my arrival, the police are coming up." My whole body felt as though it were outwardly shuddering, but bluff is a game more than one can play.

"Did Crook tell you to say that?" Gerald asked.

"Oh, I forgot," I said airily. "You didn't know he was in hospital, did you? Some villain plunged the house into darkness and then threw him down the stairs, but you wouldn't know anything about that, would you? Lucky for you, really," I went on. "If and when it gets out who was responsible, you'll never make it to the States. Twenty thousand Londoners will know the reason why. If you don't believe me," I added, casting every egg in my possession into one frail basket, "watch for yourself. Sixty seconds to countdown."

I stared at the face of the square golden watch Aubrey had given me. "Watches are for use, not for ornament," he had said when he put it on my wrist. "You want to be able to see the time without a magnifying glass." The busy little hand ticked around. I saw that Tracy was automatically following my example, his eyes fixed on the sensible timepiece strapped on his wrist. Only Gerald didn't consult a watch, because his kind doesn't have a second hand. Fifty seconds. Forty. Thirty . . .

"They must be coming on foot," said Gerald, who was standing by the window. "No cars in sight, unless you count a taxi." He turned back.

"Check!" said Tracy suddenly.

"Playing Silly Buggers, are you?" Gerald inquired.

And as though his words were a cue, the telephone began to ring.

Gerald hesitated, then lifted the receiver. Tracy and I could hear the voice as clearly as though the speaker was in the next room.

"Sorry to disturb you, Mr. Porter," said the slightly greasy accent—the commissionaire, no doubt, "but the lady's husband is here. He says he's expected."

Gerald turned to me. "What's the trick?" he demanded.

I was as flabbergasted as he. How Aubrey had surprised my secret, I couldn't imagine. I suppose I was a fool to believe I could ever keep him in the dark. My heart had been shaking ever since I came into the building, but nothing to the way it shook now.

"Shall I send the gentleman up?" the voice persisted.

"The lady's coming down," said Gerald shortly.

I turned before he could change his mind. I was between him and the door, and I was out in a flash. I heard a key turn behind me as I slammed the front door. The lift had just stopped to disgorge a passenger. A man wearing a brightly checked coat and looking as though he hadn't a care in the world came toward me.

"You said twenty minutes," he observed. "Just right. Just gave me time to finish my crossword."

He had kept the lift gate open; as I stepped in, I was aware we were being watched. Gerald must have turned the key again and opened the door. "That's not Fielding," I heard him say, and then followed a spate of foul language.

My companion paid no attention. "Got what you came for?" he said.

"I think so," I told him. I had my hands in my pockets again.

"Wait for it," said my companion. "Wait till you see Parsons."

"Parsons!" I was flabbergasted again. "But where . . . ?"

"You rang him, didn't you?"

"Yes, but—there wasn't time . . ."

"Time doesn't exist for people like him and Crook. That is, they don't allow it to be their master."

"It was a spur-of-the-minute decision," I said.

The lift stopped and my spurious husband handed me out. "I've got a taxi," he observed. "We'll go right along to Bloomsbury Street."

"He must have acted like the wind," I said. I was still unsure whether I was standing on my head or my heels.

We walked down the road and got into the taxi. "123 Bloomsbury Street," my companion said.

"I thought you were going to be Aubrey," I explained.

"Given to sudden decisions, aren't you? Still, that bit about the spur of the minute—that's what you might call a terminological inexactitude. You'd got it all worked out last night, hadn't you?"

"You mean, you knew . . . ?"

"If X didn't mind taking a chance with Mr. Crook, he wasn't going to be deterred by anyone smaller. Besides, you were snouting round here."

"Were you following me?" It was all for my security, no doubt, but I was full of indignation.

"Mr. Crook's orders. When you didn't go in, I knew you must be working out a plan."

"Did you follow me to Hambridges?"

"No need. I hung about till I saw Porter come out, so I knew you had no date for that evening. But this morning was a different matter. I was waiting around . . . When you told me you were seeing someone in the flats—where did your husband come in, by the way?—I oiled off and rang Parsons. He said the lady asked you to pick her up in twenty minutes, do just that. No earlier, because these ladies are usually slow starters, though they can go fast enough once they get going. Longest twenty minutes I've spent for quite a while," he added candidly.

"It seemed to go past like the wind. Tracy was there—Etta's first husband, I suppose her only one really. Etta was blackmailing him and his wife without the other knowing. Gerald knew, naturally."

"Didn't do his mental arithmetic carefully enough," commented my companion.

I wanted to ask what he meant by that, but I could see from his face he wasn't going to tell me. I'd better wait till I met Bill.

"What's the news about Mr. Crook?" I remembered to ask.

"Be on the warpath again any day now. Difficult to know if the police are grateful or not. When he's in hospital he can't be making trouble for them. On the other hand, it'll release quite a number of the force when he's up and about again."

Bill was waiting for us as we climbed the stairs in Bloomsbury Street. They seemed endless, but the man who'd been my watchdog tucked his hand under my arm like any husband. The workmen were just finishing clearing up. "It's worth it, lady," one of them said.

Bill was wearing a scowl and showed about as much feeling as a block of wood. He didn't ask how I was feeling or even bid me good day. "Have you got it?" he said.

I took my hands out of my pockets and laid on the table the little mini pocket tape recorder I had bought at Hambridges the night before. "It's all there," I said. "As Gerald remarked, the recorder is like the camera, it cannot lie. Hoist on his own petard." I felt slightly drunk.

"Homo sapiens has always been one up on either of them," Bill agreed.

"I don't know," I said, anxiety gnawing at my vitals once again, "if it'll satisfy the police. It seemed—so final to me . . ."

"It's not our job to satisfy the police," Bill pointed out. "Though as good citizens, Crook might think it appropriate to lend them a hand."

I thought he'd have split his sides if he could have heard Bill say that. "I still haven't got a motive," I blurted out, "but you'll say we don't have to supply that either."

"Trouble with double-crossers is it becomes a habit like taking one too many of an evening or sucking your thumb. Presently you take it for granted. Etta had been double-crossing everyone for years. Porter must have been crazy to think that sooner or later she wouldn't turn on him."

"Is that what happened?"

"I don't know, do I? But like you said, there has to be a motive. It wouldn't surprise me to know she was planning to slip off without telling him. He'd no claims on her, he wasn't her husband. But we'll let the police work that one out."

He set up the recorder. It's very strange hearing your own voice on a tape. Mine sounded insufferably condescending.

"There was a passport in her bag, and an air ticket," I recalled.

"Not our problem," Bill said calmly.

I listened to the tape. "*Is* it enough?" I asked doubtfully. While I had been in the flat in Goodwood Mansions it had seemed to me that Gerald Porter had condemned himself out of his own mouth. He couldn't deny the record, but—might a clever lawyer give it a second meaning?

"If he's got the sense he was born with, he'll plead guilty to manslaughter," Bill said. "Under extreme provocation. Probably did try to telephone from the booth in the alley and found her instrument wasn't working. He looks out, you're going away, the girl—Mrs. Tracy—has vanished. He goes in to find the place in disorder—fortunate for him that there was that flick knife in evidence, he can plead self-defense."

"He could say he found her dead," I protested. "Then if he produced the earring as evidence . . ."

"In which case why didn't he call the police right away? Answer, he'd have had to explain what he was doing there. But if he waits, as he did, he can rig himself up some alibi for the fatal time . . ."

"But I'd seen him."

"He was counting on you doing just what you did, keeping mum. Besides, even if you'd gone to the police, he only had to say he hadn't been near Klondyke Street at seven o'clock, and it was a question of which one they chose to believe. It was a darkish night, you only saw him for a moment, there was a time when you weren't absolutely sure yourself. You didn't see him come out of the alley, you didn't see him cross the road."

"Why didn't Mrs. Tracy see him?"

"She was in the tobacco shop. She wouldn't hurry, she'd want to give you a chance to get away, he'd seize his opportunity. He could hide behind the curtain or slip into the hall and up the stairs and wait till the girl was inside. It's easy to believe she didn't get in—who was there to let her in? And silence was golden for everyone and he knew it. Crook'll be interested to hear this," he added. "Next move will be up to him."

"When will he be back?" I wondered.

"Coming out tomorrow," promised Bill. "You'll be hearing from him."

I had an enormous sense of anticlimax. I don't know what I'd expected—a sounding of bells, a twanging of harps, a shaking of tambourines. It was all too quiet. "What do I do now?" I asked forlornly. "And don't tell me just wait."

"Go back and put your husband in the picture," said Bill coolly. "Someone's got to and it'll come better from you."

12

I had been explaining the situation to Aubrey. He listened with very little comment, only now and again bringing me back into line when, like Dickens' Mrs. Nickleby, I strayed off the main road.

"What I don't understand," he said finally, with the quietness that is more devastating than a storm, "is why you didn't confide in me before."

I stared back at him. "How could I? I never meant you to know. Aubrey, if you'd seen that letter—even though it was never sent—anyone, but anyone, would see it as a *cri de coeur* from a discarded mistress to her faithless lover." If I hadn't recognized my own handwriting, I could have sworn it was a forgery. Some of the phrases came swinging back into my mind. I felt myself turn crimson. "Surely you see I had to get it back at any cost? And, of course, there was Tom and his family to be considered," I wound up rather lamely. I hadn't actually given him much thought. "If that had appeared in the press . . ."

"Oh, come," said Aubrey. "You don't really believe there was any danger of that. You can't have much opinion of our press if you think they take that sort of risk. And Mrs. Porter wouldn't have taken it either. Even the most tolerant judge hasn't a good word to say for the blackmailer, and there's something called the law of libel. No, Etta Porter never intended to take that risk. That's the blackmailer's strength. They know they'll be bought off, they can make any threats they please. And what, in fact, had you to fear? You knew you were innocent of your husband's death. I knew it, you knew I knew it. A court of law had found you Not Guilty. You're like all the blackmailer's victims, Meg, you let yourself be rushed into a situation that didn't really exist."

"You didn't know Etta," I muttered. "She was quite ruthless. She didn't only use you as a weapon, she used Gavin. And any man in your shoes is bound to have some enemies. There was Mrs. French . . ." I stopped abruptly. "Aubrey, you don't think she was trying to blackmail her, too?"

"You're letting your imagination run away with you," Aubrey assured me. "What grounds had she for trying to blackmail her? If there'd been any positive evidence against Mrs. French, it would have been brought out at the trial."

"You always thought she was responsible, didn't you?" I murmured.

"I was convinced of it. But I don't think Etta Porter was blackmailing her, if only because there are complications about blackmailing someone who's in prison."

"Prison? Mrs. French? You never told me. How long have you known?"

I felt real indignation if he really did know anything and had kept it from me all this time, and I daresay that showed in my voice.

"It was when we had that trouble about Gavin," said Aubrey slowly. "I'd turned down this brief in the West because I couldn't face the thought of bad news unless you were beside me, and then we knew we weren't going to lose him, and you took him away for a few weeks' convalescence. And while I was on my own in London a solicitor I knew called Carisbrooke said he had a client who was particularly anxious I should undertake her case. Her name meant nothing to me— Mrs. Armstrong—but I hesitated when I heard the type of case it was. She was accused of having poisoned her husband. Since our marriage I've carefully avoided getting implicated in cases of this nature, it seemed to me simply common sense with the press out for any tidbits they can snatch. But Caris-brooke made such a point of it and I had nothing else on my plate at the moment, so I thought there could be no harm in my just seeing the woman."

"I wonder what made her ask for you," I speculated. "Wouldn't she be afraid of the old case coming up? But I suppose she thought if you could get me off, you could save anyone. Had she changed much?" I added.

It was a question any woman would have asked, but Aubrey looked startled. "As a matter of fact," he acknowledged, "I didn't immediately recognize her. Just had the feeling it was someone I ought to know but just couldn't place. She'd been abroad after the trial, put herself into the hands of a French plastic surgeon and he'd made a very good job of her. She'd been a handsome woman then and she was handsome still, but not in quite the same way. You remember her nose? A little too long, dominating, deep-rooted, but giving character to the face. She'd had it shortened, it was less aggressive and it toned down her personality. She'd changed the style and color of her hair, but she'd forgotten there's one thing you can't change, and that's your hands. I remember noticing them in the witness box. They didn't match the rest of her appearance. She was poised and elegant, but her hands were stubby and broad, the hands of a woman born to work. She kept them well, but she couldn't disguise their shape. She used them a lot in the box, and when I'd been talking to her for a minute, I knew I was seeing those same hands. For one thing, I don't suppose you noticed, but the third and fourth fingers are the same length."

Automatically I looked down at my own hands. "You don't miss much," I murmured. "All the same, I don't see how she could have expected you to act for her."

"Oh, as to that," said Aubrey, "she appeared to think I owed her a favor. If it hadn't been for her intervention, involuntary though it was, she assured me I shouldn't have got my verdict. Her view is that the jury was convinced she wasn't concerned in Derek Harding's death, but there was no absolute proof, so they gave you the benefit of the doubt. Which is quite a neat summing-up of the situation. Oh, she didn't anticipate any favors for free; she was quick to assure me of that. Ray's played ducks and drakes with her bank balance, she said, but even he hadn't been able to empty the till."

"Ray being . . . ?"

"Mr. Raymond Armstrong, her lawful wedded husband. He was twelve or thirteen years younger than herself, she'd met him when she was footloose. Raymond was English representative for a firm with a branch in Paris. He was no doubt infatuated by her; she had that quality, will probably have it to her dying day, though the men she'll infatuate will change—be older, more tolerant, proud of having a wife like that to display. Well, your first husband was caught by her—I don't doubt at one time she had him eating out of her hand—Ray Armstrong seems to have been the same. They got married and eventually came back to England. And there, after about three years, the inevitable happened. He was working among girls of his own age and upbringing, he shook off his infatuation and fell in love. She must have guessed it would happen. She was fifty or thereabouts, he was still in his thirties. Infidelity took place— she told me all this quite candidly—she taxed him with it, he didn't deny it, he asked for his freedom and she refused."

"And then he died?"

"Yes."

"Of poison?"

"Yes."

"She must have been mad," I protested. "She might have pulled it off once, but not even her vanity could make her think she'd succeed a second time."

"That's just where you're wrong, Meg," Aubrey corrected me. "Study the Newgate Calendar. It's jam-packed with cases of men and women who killed without ruth, practically always employing the same means each time. There was Smith with his brides in the bath; there was Neil Cream with his unfortunates; there was Landru with his unofficial brides in the forest of Gambais; there was John Christie; there was that Victorian horror Mrs. Dyer and her string of murdered infants—the same procedure employed every time. *I've fooled the people, the police, the press once, why shouldn't I do it again?*"

"Did you never even think she might be innocent?" I asked my husband.

"No more than I'd believed her innocent years ago. I thought then that a woman with nothing to hide would have come forward and told the court that Derek Harding had been in a depressed state that evening, having heard he was losing his job."

"She didn't want anyone to know she'd even met Derek," I pointed out. "How did you track her down, anyway?"

"It was something you said, when your husband asked for a second glass of sherry, that you thought he'd already had two or three before he came home. The obvious place for a man to drink at the end of the day is a bar, so I had a private agent going the rounds trying to trace your husband's movements, and eventually he came up with the name of the Cock and Fosters. The barman there had recognized a photograph; he couldn't swear to the dead man's name, but he had been in more than once with a woman who called him Derek. He didn't suppose he could identify the woman, he didn't pay any special attention, there were so many clients, but eventually we tied the pair together. Then, when she was questioned, she volunteered that it was quite easy to get sleeping tablets under the counter if you had the right contacts. How did she know that, unless she had them? It might be drawing a bow at a venture, but another man drew a bow at a venture and slew a king."

"And this time?" I said.

"I don't think she was the sort of woman who would ever forgive a slight, particularly where it involved a man who preferred another woman to herself. She told her friends that if her husband left her, she'd kill herself. The prosecution worked hard but they couldn't find anyone who had heard her say that if he deserted her, she'd kill him."

"But he was the one who died?"

"Precisely."

"What foxes me," I said, "is how Carisbrooke could have expected you to undertake her defense, knowing the part she'd played in the earlier case."

"He didn't know," explained Aubrey. "A lot of water had flowed under the bridges since Derek Harding died. She had gone abroad, where for a time she was known as Madame Barri, though there's no reason to believe she had any right to the title. M. Barri appears to have been an executive accustomed to having what he wanted and paying for it. The liaison lasted about three years, when he retired and paid the lady off, to put it crudely, quite handsomely. Then, after a while, she met this Ray Armstrong and fell for him, hook, line and sinker. So far as Carisbrooke was concerned, she had no past, no further back than Barri anyway. There was no reason why he should suspect her real identity. It was a long time ago, and he's still quite a young man.

"There's every reason to suppose that Armstrong had good reasons for wanting a quick divorce, there was never any question of his remaining with his wife. And so, one day, the neighbors are shocked to hear there's been a death at the Armstrong household, and somewhat more than surprised to know the victim isn't Mrs. Armstrong, despite her previous threats of suicide, but Armstrong himself."

"And she poisoned him?"

"Let's play it safe," suggested Aubrey, "and say she supplied the vehicle. That much she admitted. She told the sort of story in the witness box that always catches at the public imagination. She couldn't live without him, but she didn't see why she should make things easy for him. So she fell back on the good old British habit of compromise. She had these tablets—there was no secret at all about that, they were kept in an unlocked cupboard equally available to husband and wife. On the fatal night she made the coffee and dropped an overdose into one of the cups. Then she closed her eyes—this is the story she told the court—and moved the cups around on the table until she couldn't have told you which was the loaded one. Coffee's always a good vehicle, because it disguises nearly every taste. They both liked their coffee sugared, which helped things along. She claimed there was even an element of excitement in the situation. She saw her husband take one cup and drain it, and didn't know which cup it was. She drained the other. Goodbye, she told him, I daresay we shan't be seeing much more of each other. And the next morning she was as fit as the proverbial flea, and he was as dead as a coffin nail."

"And that's the story she told in the dock?" I said, incredulous and dazed. "And her counsel let her?"

"She finally got a man called Hosea; he's an unconventional fellow with a reputation for having made his way by climbing on the backs of questionable clients. He's a persuasive speaker and the jury brought in a verdict of manslaughter. There was a number of women on the jury and I heard she gained their sympathy. Armstrong was a fool," he added. "He should have known from the start that he wasn't up to her weight."

"And what do you think?" I asked him cautiously. "Strictly off the record, of course."

"Strictly off the record," said Aubrey, "I think he got the cup he was intended to get. But there's no proof, there couldn't be. It was another case of reasonable (or unreasonable) doubt. A lot depends on the personality of the prisoner. If you'd put forward a defense like that, I wouldn't have undertaken your case; with a flamboyant creature like Mrs. French (which is how I shall always think of her) there was, say, one chance in a hundred that she was telling the truth. Naturally," he added, "I'm prejudiced. I'm still convinced she murdered your husband."

"What happened to her? Did she get off again?"

"With a verdict of manslaughter? Hardly. On her own admission she had provided the means. The judge gave her a five-year sentence—afterward it was rumored that he never doubted her guilt, but it's the jury that brings in the verdict and ties the judge's hands. That was three years ago. With good behavior she should be out in a few months."

He said it so calmly, as if he were repeating the story of someone else's life, I was staggered.

"What do you suppose she'll do then?" I asked, in what I hoped sounded a callous voice. "She can't go on taking husbands—her own and other people's—and poisoning them."

He sent me a glance that made me feel ashamed, but he said coolly enough, "Oh, I think three and a half years in prison will have been time enough to teach her sense."

"What can she do?" I urged.

"If she asked my advice, I'd say find a new environment —go to Bermuda or Malta or buy a villa in Spain—you don't pay for your keep in prison—and though I understand Ray ran through a lot of her capital, it would be an investment worth while. She's the kind of woman who'll always make the best of herself and her circumstances; all she has to wait for is an elderly man, a widower perhaps, in not too robust health, and smooth his last years. Before she's sixty she could find herself a legitimate widow very comfortably off, and thereafter she could please herself."

"I never knew I'd married a cynic," I said. I really was shocked.

But Aubrey only replied, "I'd be much more shocked to hear she'd taken to good works. To date she's always acted according to her nature, and consistency, we are told, is a jewel."

I wondered, irrationally, about the girl Ray had been going to marry. I didn't suppose anyone had asked about her. "And all these years you've known this about her," I said, "and never a word to me!"

"I reminded you—we'd just got the news about Gavin—you'd had an eternity of anxiety, even if it was only five days long—did you suppose I wanted to fix your thoughts on your dead husband? Yes, of course I was always jealous of him, the man you loved before you loved me. Irrational, unfair, but I wasn't going to be the one to turn your thoughts back to him. You wanted a rest, you wanted assurance—what's a husband for if he doesn't get those things for you?"

"But it's so *interesting*," I protested. And I went on uncontrollably, "Sometimes I think the selfish husbands are the best sort to have, the ones who aren't thinking of your feelings all the time."

But Aubrey only said that all husbands were selfish, and presumably wives preferred them that way or they'd have done something about it.

"You're talking just like Mr. Crook," I accused him, and he laughed and said I couldn't pay him a greater compliment.

Next day I went to see Mr. Crook, who was still in hospital.

"A more reasonable patient might have been allowed home by now," said Sister severely. "I'm sure beds are in short enough supply. But Mr. Crook will be swarming up a tree after a villain almost before he's found his feet, if we give him a chance."

"The Turks had the right idea," he greeted me. He seemed as ebullient as ever. The dark bruise on his forehead looked as triumphant as a decoration. "Shut their women up. They know they're not safe on their own. If you wanted to commit suicide, Sugar, what was wrong with a bottle of aspirin?"

"I didn't want to commit suicide, and I wasn't in the least

interested in avenging Etta, and I knew you had Bill Parsons and the faceless army on your side, but that still left Mr. James."

"Mr. James ain't our problem, Sugar."

"He's *my* problem," I assured him. "And he was pushed. I can't prove it, but . . ."

"Oh, I believe you," said Mr. Crook agreeably, "same like I was pushed. Gerald seems the pushing kind. What's more, there was a lady on the same side of the road, and she thought he was pushed. Told the copper on duty, and when he warned her not to obstruct a bobby on the job, she romped along to the copper shop and gave a very good description, fits your Mr. Porter to a T. A silly fellow," said Mr. Crook indulgently, "making himself conspicuous with that watch chain, though, mind you, it had its uses."

"Will the tapes be any use to the police?"

"Might be if they could find them, but they ain't holding Gerald on a blackmail charge. Just simple murder. I'll tell you something, Sugar, I'll lay he was as pleased as Punch when he thought of that watch. Made him look like a lord mayor on Saturday afternoon, only lord mayors like to be recognized, and chaps like Gerald 'ud do better to follow the example of the Tar Baby, who laid low and said nuffin'."

"What about the woman who gave evidence?" I inquired anxiously.

"We-ell. No evidence, see. She was out with her husband . . ."

"Didn't *he* see anything?"

"Well, Sugar"—Mr. Crook's voice was deprecating—"he was a husband, and husbands don't like bein' dragged at the tail of wifie's chariot. Didn't see anyone special, he says, lots of people on the pavement, anyone might have slipped, especially an old codger like that."

"He's got it wrong," I said. "Old people are twice as careful as the young, they need to be, they're so much more vulnerable. And if Mr. James was really going to the police . . ."

"What did he think he could tell them?"

I could see Mr. Crook really wanted to know. "Gerald had dropped hints about having some hold over me, something about uncovering skeletons. I suppose he thought he'd frighten the old man off. And, of course, he could have backed up my story about Gerald being in the garden. Mrs. Day didn't see him, or anyway, not clearly enough to know him again."

Mr. Crook shook his head. "That's the trouble with these chaps who grew up in the welfare state, Nanny holds your hand all the way. Old codgers like your Mr. James, and Bill and me, we learned to stand on our own feet while these others are still getting their vitamin tablets from a hopeful state, and if we cracked an ankle or broke a kneecap, we taught ourselves to hop. And if we lost both feet, we learned to walk on our hands. No, the old boy meant what he said."

"And he'd have made the police listen," I insisted.

"I wouldn't be surprised," Mr. Crook agreed. "And Gerald couldn't afford to have the fuzz taking any further interest in him."

"I'm still convinced I did see him that night when I came out of Etta's apartment."

"Nice to know there's one point on which we agree," said Mr. Crook amicably.

"So why was he there unless he meant to go in?"

"Who says he didn't mean to go in? Probably telling the truth when he says he tried to get her on the buzzer from the alley, then when he got no reply, he beetled over. You were out of sight, Mrs. T. was still in the shop, in he went."

"And what happened then?"

"Well, we don't know, do we?" said Mr. Crook. "But he'll sing. Oh yes, he will. He'll sing like a canary bird. Bill's probably got the right end of the stick when he says she was probably trying to double-cross him. If she was going to make a new start in a new country, she probably wouldn't want all that old load of cods-wallop tagging after her. He had no claim on her, remember; he wasn't her husband, they didn't draw the line at much, but apparently they jibbed at bigamy. She didn't even take his name by Deed Poll, so far as we can find out. Well, it'll be his word against the police, no proof either way. Bill's probably right, he'll get a few years. One thing, you can't get a suspended sentence in cases like this, so, though we'll be supporting him for some time to come, he'll have to draw in his horns. Stir should be quite a happy hunting ground for him," he went on casually. "Wonderful how much you can learn when you share a fellow's cell for months on end."

"What shocks me," I said, "is that Tracy was prepared to go along with him in this. He knew what Gerald was like, he knew he and Etta had been soaking his wife as well as himself, but when it came to the crunch, he was prepared to back up Gerald."

Crook gave me a long, wondering stare. "Dames bug me, honest they do," he said. "What else did you expect? Nothing in it for Walter by siding with you. Mind you, I don't say he don't have a very warm feeling for the little woman, but he'd be less than human if he didn't feel the pull of her half-million dollars. A rum will," he went on, in the tone of a man who can understand and pardon even the rummiest occurrence provided it's not an Englishman behind it, "she was to get this money on her twenty-sixth birthday or when she'd been married for two years. Two years since they went through the ceremony would have been up next month, but of course she'd never actually been married."

"She's married now," I said.

"Didn't lose any time, did he? She's twenty-two now, they'll have to wait their two years. Still, it takes most chaps longer than that to get half a million greenbacks. You do see his point, don't you, Sugar? Even the Good Book only tells you to love your neighbor as yourself, and they loved themselves unto the death, Etta's death, and but for an interferin' snoopy Providence, yours."

"It still seems hardly possible," I said. "That this sort of thing should happen to me again? Don't they say lightning never strikes in the same place twice?"

"Well, now you know that ain't true. An old hand like me could have told you that from the start. You don't suppose this is the first time I've come tip over arse on my own staircase? But that don't mean it won't happen again next week."

"It was Gerald who killed old Mr. James, I'm certain of it. Do you mean to say he's going to get away with it?"

"I mean, we ain't judge, jury, nor yet the fuzz. You weren't there, your Mrs. Day wasn't there. There was a verdict of accidental death. Your husband ain't going to thank you for trying to raise the matter again, and anyway, they've got Porter in safe custody, and you can't do anything to help old Mr. James now."

"Vengeance is mine," I muttered, and Crook nearly reduced me to hysterics by saying, "You're talking to a lawyer, Sugar, or had you forgotten? The law don't acknowledge the right of private vengeance to any individual. Lucky in a way you're hitched up to a lawyer, too. Can't afford to be too personal—though just as well for Porter he's under lock and key."

"Aubrey knows all about it," I said. "I told him last night."

For the first time I saw I'd scored a bull's-eye. Mr. Crook was looking at me with an air not far removed from reverence. He raised an imaginary hat. "I dips me lid," he said simply. "Me, I'd as soon face a raging tiger."

Someone came walking down the corridor toward the sideward where Crook had been stowed. Sister said she wasn't going to chance a rough house on her ward when it got around who the latest arrival was. They hadn't managed to keep out Bill Parsons, but most of the other would-be visitors had been fielded at the hospital gate. Bill had been right when he said the first thing Crook would see was a dirty great policeman with a notebook.

"And a lot of good that did him," commented Crook. "What could I tell him? I was coming downstairs and I tripped in the dark—it ain't the first time and it won't be the last. When I have to start asking for police protection, I can hang up me hat on a pensioner's hook. If they think some human agency was involved, let them put a name to him. It's what we pay them for, ain't it?"

The footsteps stopped and the door opened. Aubrey stood on the threshold. "According to Sister, visiting hours are over," he said. "No need to ask how you're getting on, Crook. You'll beat the Recording Angel one of these days. Meantime, I've come for my wife."

I was almost out of the door before I remembered to turn and say goodbye to Mr. Crook. It was like looking through the wrong end of a telescope. I saw a tiny figure in the bed; the bruise didn't look like a decoration any more, just a common or garden bruise. I wasn't being ungrateful to him, and I'd never stop admiring him, but this was my husband and I was going home.